WOODY AND JUNE VERSUS THE SIEGE

WOODY AND JUNE VERSUS THE SIEGE

WOODY AND JUNE VERSUS THE APOCALYPSE, EPISODE 12

ROBERT J. MCCARTER

LITTLE HUMMINGBIRD PUBLISHING

WOODY AND JUNE
VERSUS
THE APOCALYPSE

Woody and June versus the Siege

Woody and June versus the Apocalypse, Episode 12

Copyright © 2022 by Robert J. McCarter

Cover photography © HHLtDave5, depositphoto.com

"Zombies Ahead" image by ducu59us

Version 1.0, January 2023

ISBN: 978-1-941153-71-0

Find out more about this book at: WoodyAndJune.com

Visit Robert's website at: www.RobertJMcCarter.com

Published by:

Little Hummingbird Publishing

P.O. Box 23518

Flagstaff, AZ 86002

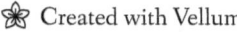 Created with Vellum

CHAPTER ONE

IT IS day thirty of Woody and June and Dallas versus the Apocalypse and day four of the zombie siege. It's my first day sitting up since we got here after I succumbed to the infection from all those zombie scratches I got back in Winslow. I feel that fresh, hopeful feeling you feel when you've crossed the line on being really sick and are actually getting better.

I am so very weak and light-headed and the now-healing scratches are starting to itch and my head still aches from where I was pistol-whipped and I'm so hungry, but compared to what I was going through, I am feeling well enough to sing and dance about it. Except, I'm way too weak for that and we're stuck up in this cell tower tree-house with the thousands-strong zombie population of Winslow milling below us, wanting to eat us.

The late spring morning is cool and the sky is a beautiful robin's egg blue. I'm propped up in a corner, my backpack behind me as a pillow and a sleeping bag wrapped around me, getting my first good look at the place.

This was clearly built by a survivor, fifty feet up in a cell tower between Winslow and Holbrook, Arizona. It's a triangular platform about twelve feet across attached to the zigzagging metal supports of the cell tower made up of a patchwork of wood of various types along with a few metal signs, probably stuff scrounged from the area. But it's strong with low walls three feet tall, an opening on one side where the ladder runs up the cell tower, and a few storage bins built into one wall.

Getting this much wood and other materials up here and building something safe took an enormous amount of effort. There is no clue who this survivor was, no personal effects left although it was stocked with canned goods, a propane stove with fuel, and a couple jerry cans of water.

The effect is at once comforting and also unnerving. On the floor there's crappy particle board that's obviously been out in the weather too long right next to a "One Way" sign. Bits of an old billboard shouting about its great unlimited cell plan make up part of a wall. The foundation of the treehouse is made up largely of two-by-fours and even two-by-sixes, but there are other stretches of structural supports where the boards are not long enough and sistered together, some of different sizes.

It's a miracle, really, that we have a place that we can rest and recover, but it creaks and is made up of such a jumble of material it's hard to really trust. And it's a bit of an eyesore with some of the wood bare but much of it painted a variety of colors, not to mention the odd road sign or two.

The food and the water are a miracle too. We didn't prepare this place—it was likely Talia. We've been boiling the water and it hasn't made us sick which is a huge relief after the group of brand-new Zs we encountered back at the North Rim. They had drunk water infected by the fungus and turned.

June and Dallas are at the other end of the treehouse having a whispered conversation. It doesn't bother me, I'm still so proud and happy to be sitting up, to be alive, to have beat the infection from the scratches and to be back in the land of the living.

June is petite and athletic with ocean-blue eyes, short black hair, olive skin, and is the love of my life. The girl of my dreams that I didn't meet until the world went to shit. She nursed me back to life, but I think the distance that opened up between us after she saved me in Winslow is still there.

Dallas is taller and curvier with shoulder-length brown hair and a sharp tongue and a quick wit dressed in an obnoxiously pink down coat.

June and I met thirty days ago. Dallas joined us eleven days later. We've been through so much I feel like I've known these women all my life, and I certainly trust them with my life.

They keep whispering and glancing at me, like they are sizing me up, accessing me.

"Are you wondering what I want for breakfast?" I ask, my voice still weak. I don't wait for a reply. "Eggs Benedict would be lovely, thank you, and don't spare the hollandaise."

I end with a smile, the most charming one I can manage. This is not a laugh-worthy effort, I'm not up to it, but I am hoping for an ironic chuckle. They are both really serious about something, and while the apocalypse is full of serious moments, I am dedicated to it having some light ones.

June sighs and walks two steps and squats down in front of me, zipping her blue jacket up to the neck. "There's something we should show you," she says, biting her lower lip briefly.

"Before breakfast?" I ask with a smile.

One eyebrow arches. "You are feeling better," she says.

I nod. "Sitting up like a real boy. My goal for the day is to drink enough water so that I can pee on the Zs below."

My gaze drifts to my hands and I have to tell you that looking at them kind of freaks me out. The scratches from the Zs are long and ragged and cover my hands and my forearms. I got them when I was surrounded by the horde below us in Winslow after we saved Dallas, when they were all grasping for me, trying to eat me, when June dragged me out with our truck.

They are scabbed up now, all red and angry, and there are a lot of them. On my palms, on the back of my hands, up my forearms. Deep, ragged, and jagged. It looks like they are going to heal now, but I'll be left with scars, and plenty of them.

I can smell the Zs below us and it takes me right back there. I had my baseball bat and was fending them off for all I was worth, fighting even though I knew there was no way out until June risked herself and rammed the truck into the mass of them, getting close enough for me to have a fighting chance.

I had to fight my way to the truck, ignoring those behind me. I felt bites through my army surplus jacket, hands grasping at me, so many hands. I dropped the bat and shed the coat to get them off me and held onto the grill while June dragged me out, while the zombies grasped at me, leaving me with a few errant scratches on my shoulders and back where the Zs ripped through my shirt.

I lost my army surplus jacket and the seeds I had in the pocket that were my beacon for the future, that represented finding a place peaceful enough to stop running and grow things. I lost my Diamondbacks baseball cap, which was my link to the past. And I lost my bat which was kind of my identity. I had survived until I met June with mostly just a bat to fight off the Zs.

I had lost all my talismans that day, but I had kept my life.

June's cool hand takes my chin and gently lifts it up as a small smile plays on her round face. "Are you with me, Woody?" she asks, her voice gentle.

"Always," I say, shoving the thoughts back. I need time, time to heal, time to process, but mostly time to figure out how the hell we get out of here.

She nods. "Good. There is something you should see."

I look around, peering over the low wall of our temporary home at the high desert around us. The land is mostly flat with pale, sandy soil, a mix of old brown weeds and newer ones greening up from the scant spring rain, some of them looking like they will someday become tumbleweeds, and a scattering of small, scraggly trees. South of us is I-40, two divided lanes in each direction, eerily quiet. Beyond the highway is a snaking swath of green that stands out in the dry desert marking the pathway of the Little Colorado River. To the north the land gently rises and the horizon is decorated with low mesas.

"No," she says. "It's here. It's a... a video."

"What?" I ask. I'm confused and then notice that Dallas is standing right behind June holding a tablet computer. She's only putting a little weight on her left foot, but it looks like her ankle is healing. That's good news. And she doesn't have handcuffs on her ankles or wrists, so they figured out a way to get those off.

"A video," Dallas says, "from the queen bitch of the desert."

Talia. Dallas has taken to calling her "queen bitch of the desert." Talia is June's ex and the psychotic, petty, wannabe warlord that's been chasing us all over Northern Arizona and maneuvering us into the worst circumstances as part of her "game."

Talia who captured Dallas and chained her to a statue in Winslow precipitating the rescue there that ended up with me surrounded by zombies.

Talia who captured me at a car dealership after we escaped the Winslow trap, knocked me out, and cuffed me to the fence of this cell tower and forced us into this predicament.

Talia is the reason that both June and Dallas have bruises on their faces that are still healing. Why I have a scab on my forehead and a healing bullet hole in my left arm. And why I got all these zombie scratches and almost died and became a zombie.

It all tumbles into place. This cell tower being stocked with us under siege by the Zs was part of her plan, part of her "game." This is the latest trap and the latest test.

My heart hammers, making my head hurt worse where she knocked me out, but it's nothing compared to what it used to be.

"Let's see it," I say.

June gives me a long appraising look and Dallas gives me a grim nod. Even the thought of watching this video brings the past few days of trauma to the front of my mind and my heart starts galloping in my chest. I nod my ascent, my mouth now too dry to say anything more.

CHAPTER TWO

I'M HOLDING the tablet and June and Dallas are sitting close to me. The freeze-frame shows Talia standing in the desert, her spine erect and her shoulders thrown back. She's tall, about six feet, and is lean and wiry, dressed in a blue down jacket. Her sandy blond hair is pulled back into her usual ponytail and the sides of her head are shaved, the dark ink of a tattoo showing on her neck.

Behind her I can see a line of green and suspect this was filmed near here, although the Little Colorado runs along I-40 most of the way between Winslow and Holbrook.

I'm hesitating. I don't want to see her face, much less hear her voice. I don't want to know what she has to say. It feels like playing the video will make what's going on more real. By the way June and Dallas are acting, it seems likely it will.

I rack my brain looking for some kind of joke that will lighten the mood, that will let us forget for a moment that thousands of Zs are milling below us and we have limited supplies and no way out.

I take a deep breath that comes out as a long sigh.

"Just hit play, Woody," Dallas says. She is impatient, but there's an unusual gentleness to her voice, so I know it must be bad.

I nod and tap the tablet and the image jumps and Talia starts talking.

"Is it rolling? Okay. Here we go." Her thin lips form a smile but it's a scary little thing, her light southern accent grating against my nerves. "Hello, my June-bug and Dallas. I am so sorry about Woody. He was in a bad way when we met, and while I'm not sure, I doubt that he survived. Those scratches of his..." She pauses and shrugs like she's talking about something silly and inconsequential, like rain ruining a picnic. "Well, I doubt that he made it.

"And if he did, well, hello Mr. Woodpecker, you are one lucky sonofabitch, which you've been proving to me over and over."

She takes a step towards the camera, her hazel eyes intense, and licks her lips like she's about to tuck into a bucket of fried chicken. "But do a girl a favor, Woody, and just die, okay?"

She backs up and kicks at the ground which I can see is dirty blacktop. "You girls have done well. Remarkably well. I don't know if you all want to see it, but there's some video of your exploits here shot by the drones. Dallas, you'll want to see your ride down Route 66 chained to that statue, sparks flying as the truck drags you along, you cursing the whole damn way. It's a real hoot."

She pauses and chuckles, quietly shaking her head before looking back at the camera. "You should have died today, Dallas, you traitorous bitch. After all I did for you, taking you in, making you part of my company. You little—" Talia turns her head and visibly gets herself under control, but I can see her fists are clenched. It looks like the feelings between Talia and Dallas are mutual.

She turns back to the camera and smiles another one of her scary smiles. "It should be down to the happy couple. I never thought they'd figure a way to save you... by taking the whole damn statue."

She moves forward again, a couple of steps until her face is filling the screen. I can see dark circles under her eyes and I am glad that she's been at least losing sleep during all of this madness. "But it turned out okay, all praise to Gaia and Jesus. Woody's probably dead and one of you had to put a bullet in his head. And now you two are stuck up in that cell tower. And that's good. I got some business to attend to. You've got supplies for two weeks and that should be enough time. I'll be back and we can resume our little game."

She smiles and I swear she's trying to smile genuinely, but it just freaks me out.

"Until then, ladies," she says, stepping back. "Enjoy your accommodations."

The video jerks back to the beginning, but I tap the tablet and stop it. June is stiff next to me, breathing hard. Dallas has a freaked-out look on her face.

"This is good news," I say, my voice barely above a whisper.

"What?" June asks.

"She thinks I'm dead," I say. "She thinks we can't escape. We have some time."

"Unless this is a part of her damn game," Dallas says.

I nod. "It could be, but think about it. Talia took over Brown's group in Flagstaff so quickly, put so much energy into capturing us and then this insane game, she must have internal issues or maybe she has a conflict with another tribe. She couldn't keep this insane game up."

"Just like you told me on the way to Winslow," June says. She's got her arms wrapped around her chest, my fearless June only afraid of one person in this whole world.

"So what do we do?" Dallas asks. "How the hell do we escape the zombie horde of the century down there and get away?"

I shake my head. "One step at a time. What's for breakfast?"

CHAPTER THREE

TALIA'S CONFIDENCE is well founded. There are thousands of Zs below us and we are the only brains in town. They are all starving and we are what they eat. Sometime while I was out of it, the Zs knocked down the fence and are milling around the cell tower in a mass roughly 150 feet in diameter.

They know we are here, and unless their collective fresh-brains radar detects a better meal, they are not going anywhere. Starving Zs congregate together, the fungus that has taken them over somehow forming a collective being and amplifying their ability to detect the living. Kind of like those radio telescopes in New Mexico.

You know, the ones in the movie *Contact* that found signs of alien life. Makes me wonder if that's what this is, alien life. Like the fungus hitched a ride on a meteor and is dutifully wiping out the dominant species in its attempt to take over that planet.

I add that to the other theories of the fungal zombie apocalypse. I have two. First, time travelers engineered the spoors and sent them back because we were such dumbasses about climate change and the future is hell.

Second, that it's aliens that did the same thing for the same reason, basically, to save the planet.

And June's theory, which is that the planet itself did it. That this fungus is the creation of Gaia, the sentient planet, and she did it to save herself.

All of these theories except the new one have something in common—dumbass humanity and how we were screwing up the planet.

But I don't really like the last theory. Not that it doesn't work if you can take the leap to believing the planet has some level of consciousness, but because it's heavily influenced by Talia.

But how the zombie apocalypse came to be is not really important or relevant to our current plight, but it is the kind of thing you think about when you have time on your hands because you are stuck in a cell tower treehouse under siege by thousands of Zs.

We have breakfast after the video and I am, frankly, pretty freaked out. Talia could see that I was infected and she expected me to die. She was celebrating my death on the video. She also expected June and I to get stuck up in this treehouse before we figured out a way to save Dallas. How many steps ahead had she planned?

My breakfast is instant oatmeal, cinnamon apple, made with hot water from the little two-burner camp stove. June delivers it with a grin, steam curling up into the cold air, the sweet smell of cinnamon briefly overcoming the fetid stench of the horde.

"Eat slow," she says.

I am so hungry I want to shove it in and follow it up with six more bowls. But that would be stupid. I would get sick.

I am the only one having oatmeal, probably because I have been so sick. June and Dallas gnaw on some dried meat. The shapes are ragged and varied, not the tube crap you get at the convenience store.

We sit in a triangle on the hard wooden floor of the treehouse, they in their jackets and me wrapped up in the sleeping bag, not having a jacket anymore.

"What's the plan?" Dallas asks with a nod, once I had a few bites and it looks like I am going to keep it down.

"You guys take inventory yet?" I ask.

June nods. "Food and water for ten or twelve more days if we are very careful, the stove, some fuel, cooking supplies, the tablet, two sleeping bags, a tarp, some rope, and what we hauled up in our backpacks."

I take another bite, letting the sugary warmth linger. Normally I'd want the jerky, but my body is starved for carbs. I need some energy.

"Did you search for electronics?" I ask. "Cameras or listening devices?"

Their eyes widen and they shake their heads. I wouldn't put it past Talia to do something like that. A small solar-powered mic and transmitter so she could have someone keep tabs on us.

"Have you seen any drones?" I ask.

"No," Dallas says.

I nod. That doesn't mean there haven't been any. I take another bite and a groan of simple pleasure escapes me. I never imagined a bowl of instant oatmeal could taste this good.

"Do you and the oatmeal need a room?" Dallas asks, her brow furrowed.

I grin at her. "Maybe. Any coffee in the supplies, because me and coffee would definitely need a room."

"Just tea," June says. "Want some?"

I nod. I could use a little caffeine to jump-start my brain.

June soon comes back with a bag of Lipton tea in an enameled camping cup which must have been part of the supplies here. It's too hot to hold so she sits it down next to me.

"Okay," I begin. "We must assume we are being watched and we are being listened to."

They both nod.

"That any plan we come up with will be known by Talia," I continue.

They nod again.

"That any plan we come up with has been anticipated by Talia."

"Boy, Woody," Dallas says, ripping a chunk of jerky off the piece she's been working on. "You are sure making me glad you survived."

"How's your ankle?" I ask.

She shrugs and pulls up her pant leg. I can see that the ankle is wrapped in an ace bandage and her hiking boot is barely on. "Can't really walk on it yet," she says, "but it's getting there."

I look at June. "Any injuries slowing you down?"

She shakes her head. She's eyeing me like she's worried that I might relapse at any moment, like this is a brief rally before the end.

"Okay," I begin. "About ten days of food left, Dallas can't walk, I can't stand, and there is a good chance we are bugged. Does that about sum it up?"

I blow on the tea and take a scalding sip. Before the apocalypse, I wasn't much of a tea drinker, but the earthy flavor is so good in that moment that I completely reconsider my previous shunning of tea.

They don't answer and I can see in their faces that they are not taking my assessment very well, but I'm buoyed by my return to the land of the living and I am, despite it all, hopeful.

I lean forward and signal them to come close. They lean in until our heads are almost touching.

"We have to find the bug," I whisper, "or be confident there isn't one. And Dallas and I have to heal up. But there is a way out of this, I know it."

"How do you know?" June whispers.

"Because, Talia thinks she thought of everything," I whisper with a smile. "But no one's that good. No one can think of everything."

CHAPTER FOUR

THERE IS NO BUG. I can't believe it, but Talia didn't bug us. The kind of bug she needed wouldn't have stayed hidden through our searching.

The treehouse cabinets were emptied and everything searched. June climbed down the ladder and searched the underside of our home. We searched the short walls and the cell tower above us.

The bug would have to have a mic, a transmitter, and a solar charger. It would have to. And a battery for the night. The theoretical listener would have to be far enough away to be out of range of the horde's fresh brains radar, and that means power. The mic could be hidden, the transmitter might be hideable, but not the solar charger and battery. And there would be some kind of wire from the charger to the transmitter and mic.

Talia didn't bug us.

That was the first day of my return to the land of the living. Oatmeal, naps, and doing what I could to help with the search. Oh, and I did live my dream and consumed enough liquids so that I got to pee on the zombie horde.

It wasn't particularly satisfying seeing how they didn't seem to be bothered by it at all, although the recipients of my gift did stir a little bit.

We talk about escape again after dark, my belly warm from a broth made of water and the jerky. June is getting me back into food slowly. I want more, but I don't have the strength to fight for it yet.

June's been distant today in an attentive way. Checking in on me, getting me things, but like she's my nurse not my girlfriend. I'm well enough for this to bother me, but not well enough to do anything about it.

I almost died. I would have without her. She must be reconsidering our relationship because of that. What else could it be?

The Zs are quieter now that it's dark, just a few of them snarling below, their putrid scent filling the air.

"Escape plans," I begin. "No idea too crazy, let's hear them." We are all leaning against one side of the treehouse and the conversation has died down.

There is silence in the darkness and it is understandable. The zombies are centered around the tower, a mass of hungry, undead eating machines roughly 150 feet in diameter. We have guns, but not enough bullets. We have some time, but not that much.

I start talking to break the silence. "Let's start with some math," I begin. "Say four thousand Zs and twelve hours of daylight a day and ten days, that gives us 120 hours. We would have to find a way to kill... let's see, a little over thirty an hour to clear them all out."

They are both still silent. It's really dark so I can't see much. We agreed to not use lights in case there is a distant observer.

"Umm...." Dallas begins. "How the hell do we do that?"

I shrug my shoulders. "No clue, but let's think it through. Not because it's a great idea but because we need to start thinking about the problem."

"Okay," June says tentatively. "That's about two minutes per Z. Or if two of us worked it at the same time, one minute per Z."

"Right," I say. "We don't have enough bullets and I've only got one stick of dynamite in my pack."

"You've got one in there?" Dallas asks.

"Yeah," I say. "For emergency purposes."

"This is kinda an emergency," she says.

"But we've got a 150-foot-diameter mass of them," I say. "The dynamite will take out, maybe, a six-foot diameter of them."

"What about nails," June says, "like you used for the suicide vest?"

"That'll help," I say. "We can get some from the treehouse, we'd have to partially deconstruct it and we'd have to hope that shrapnel doesn't hit us, but maybe that would get us to a ten-foot radius of Zs gone."

We go on in that vein for a while. A combination of methodical killing of Zs and the one stick of dynamite. I still have my pink hand weight from when June and I met, but it's not effective enough. We need something we can easily take them out with from above.

But there's nothing in the treehouse that makes sense. If we get low enough to use knives, we are in serious danger.

There are some fanciful ideas like using the tarp to create a hang glider and flying down or stripping out the wire of the cable that goes up the tower and creating long ropes out of it and swinging from the tower like Tarzan until we are beyond the diameter of the Zs and run away.

"Didn't they cover themselves in zombie guts in that TV show?" Dallas asks. It is much later and the ideas are getting sillier. "And then the Zs didn't know they were living."

"They did," I say. "And it worked... on the show, that is."

"But..." June says, prompting me to continue.

"It doesn't work with the real thing," I say. "Their fresh-meat radar isn't based on smell. I know this for sure."

There's a story there, they both know it, but they let it go. We all have enough stories of the apocalypse to fill our nightmares up for the rest of our lives.

"Shoes..." Dallas says slowly. "What if we had shoes with long spikes on them. We go down the ladder and stomp 'em in the head. We could easily get one every two minutes that way."

It's not a bad idea. "Except only June is healthy enough," I say.

"So," June says. "That's no reason to not try." Her tone is a little strident.

"You're right," I say, because I don't want conflict. And because she is right. Even if we can't get rid of all of them, lessening the horde is worth doing. "But not shoes. Besides not having the spikes, if we did, they would be able to grab onto your legs, and what if a spike gets caught? Shoes are not safe enough."

"What then?" June asks. She's a warrior. She's tired of sitting around. She's probably tired of taking care of me.

"We scrounge a long piece of wood from the treehouse here," I say. "Sharpen the end and you have a disposable spear."

"Now that's a plan," Dallas says.

"We start at first light," June says.

That night I sleep alone in the sleeping bag. I'm too exhausted for it to keep me awake long, but it does bother me. Because we only have two sleeping bags. Because June and I were sharing one while I was sick. Because it is the clearest sign yet that something had come between us.

CHAPTER FIVE

THAT NEXT MORNING after a brief meal, we get to work on the spear. My brain has been turning it over since we talked and I have a better plan.

We scrounge a one-by-one board from the railing of the treehouse. It was hammered in and we don't have a hammer so it takes time and careful work with knives to pry it loose.

I feel like an invalid. I am stronger but it's still a pretty accurate description, so I just supervise that part from a sitting position. I can stand now but not for long.

The board is eight feet long, which is fine. After they get it down, I go to work on it. Sharpening one end and notching the other, wrapping a rope around it and attaching a carabiner to the end of the rope.

We can't lose the spear. The idea is that June will be clipped into the ladder as she spears and the spear will be clipped in so if she drops it, we don't lose it. Or if it gets stuck in some Z's skull we can retrieve it.

We don't have a lot of usable wood up here so we need to make it count.

There's a fire in June's blue eyes as she takes the spear, clips it to her belt, and goes down the ladder. We have an insane plan—kill four thousand or so Zs by hand—but it's a plan.

It relies on the fact that Talia is not monitoring us. It gambles that Talia does not come back too soon, that Dallas and I have time to heal, that some other calamity does not fall upon us in the meantime.

When I said it last night it was just an opener, to get the conversation going. I never expected it to turn into something real.

After all the breathless escapes since we ran into Talia at the 40s, the pace of this is strange. Slow and methodical instead of adrenaline filled and desperate. It's the only pace I can currently manage, but it still feels strange.

Dallas gets to work on loosening another one-by-one board while I sit near the ladder and gaze down the tower.

We are about fifty feet up and I see the mass respond to June coming closer. They don't look up, but the ones near the ladder start to stir and the mass of them press closer. They sense their meal arriving.

There are some gaps in the mass of Zs below where the small utility building is and random gear that used to make this cell tower work.

I hear June's boots on the metal ladder, the dull ringing a rhythmic accompaniment to the snarling and snapping. I feel the vibration of it through the tower. I smell the Zs, not that we can ever get away from that. My nose has adjusted somewhat, but it's still bad. So bad that the lovely taste of my cinnamon oatmeal breakfast is soon replaced with a moldy taste because the smell is so strong.

This is my first serious look at the Zs, and the size of the horde is breathtaking—and not just because of the stench. The idea of spearing them one at a time is more than a little overwhelming.

June clips herself in and then unclips the spear from her belt and clips it to the ladder. She pauses, the spear held at the ready in her hand, and I get it.

This feels like that dude from mythology that kept rolling the rock up the hill only to have it roll back down again and he has to start over. I don't remember his name, sis-something, but that myth kinda captures what we are trying to do. How is this even possible?

I know. I did the math. Numbers don't lie, but it doesn't *feel* possible.

Holding on to the ladder with one hand, she hefts the spear, finding the right place to grip it, and stabs down. I hear the faint crack of breaking bone over the snarling, which is only getting louder now that she is down there.

One Z goes down.

And then two. And then three.

And it took about a minute. The spear is heavy enough to make this hard work, but a spark of hope ignites.

She gets the next two in about a minute and then one the minute after that before stopping and examining the end of the spear. It's taking more than one thrust now, the spear seeming to deflect off the Zs' heads more often than not.

My perspective is not a great one, the ladder is in the way and I'm above the action, but I can see enough of her movements to figure out what she's doing.

"What's wrong?" I call down.

"Not sharp anymore," she calls back.

Of course. A pointed piece of wood versus bone and the wood is going to lose. Just as quickly as it sparked, the hope sputters out.

June goes at it for a few more minutes, and gets a few more Zs, but now she's more crushing their skulls than piercing them, and that's much harder work.

A knife would work a lot better, but we don't have reliable means of attaching it.

"Everything okay?" Dallas asks. She's still working on prying another board loose. "How many has she taken out?"

"Nine," I say.

"Yes!" Dallas says doing a fist pump, the hope alive in her.

"The point is dull now," I say. "She's having to use a lot more force and is basically crushing their skulls now. It's too hard to keep it up."

Dallas pauses and catches my eye. "So let's reinforce it with something. We've got plenty of strange crap up here."

And then the hope sparks in me again. "We've got canned food, right?" I ask.

She nods. "Lots, why?"

"Because you are brilliant, Dallas," I say.

She gives me a puzzled smile. "You are right. I am brilliant. I have no idea what I did, but I am sure it was brilliant."

I shout down and call June up.

CHAPTER SIX

I'M IGNORING the little sparks of hope now.

For one thing, I'm tired. For another, I think hope can be problematic sometimes.

Like hoping that this crazy plan of spearing one Z at a time will get us out of here. Like hoping that we get this done before Talia comes back. Like hoping whatever is between June and me can be solved with one conversation.

The higher hope takes you on one of the particulars, the farther you crash when it doesn't turn out the way you wanted.

And isn't that what this kind of hope is? Wanting things to turn out as you imagine it will. Needing things to turn out that way. But the world just doesn't work that way and it sure as hell doesn't post-apocalypse.

That doesn't mean that I don't have hope. I do, but it's not specific. I have hope that we will escape and that gives me energy to keep trying. I have hope that June and I can work out what is between us, but I am not deluding myself into thinking that it will be easy or simple or quick.

I have hope for the big picture, but I have to let go of wanting any of our ideas to work out the way we think they will.

This is about survival. Avoiding the little hopes also avoids the little despairs. And those little despairs that come when things don't work out can add up real quick.

"How was it?" I ask when June gets back to the treehouse and hands me the spear.

She shrugs and is breathing hard, sweat beaded on her forehead. "Not bad at first," she says, "but it got hard."

For June to say that tells me it got very hard.

That's okay. It's early in our first day of the plan. I've got some empty tin cans and I get to work on the spear while June helps Dallas pry off the second board.

The end of the spear is blunted and covered with zombie goo, dark red, almost black, with strands of white fungus. I carve a new point, scraping off the goo, and then start in with the metal.

It's slow work. I am trying to armor the point with a tin can and attach it so it won't just fall off.

First, I use the can opener on my multi-tool and take off the bottom of the can. I then flatten it by stomping on it. I have to stand up for this and am a bit light-headed, but do okay holding onto the treehouse railing.

A hacksaw would be really nice, but that is gone with our truck and everything that was in it when Talia blew it up.

I take the can and undo the stomp and press it down in the other direction so there are folds every 90 degrees or so. I need to cut the metal but don't have the proper tools.

I end up alternating between the two folds back and forth over and over, weakening the metal at the seams. I get some work gloves from my pack, the last thing I need is to cut my hands, the zombie scratches are bad enough and itching like crazy.

This is slow work. My hands are so beat up I have to be extra careful, but I eventually get the can cut through on one of those seams.

I look up and June and Dallas are staring at me. The second spear is carved and notched and has a cord and carabiner attached. This is enough activity that I am finally feeling warm without the sleeping bag.

"What?" I ask.

June bites her lip and Dallas's forehead furrows.

"Umm..." Dallas begins. "We're just wondering what the hell you are doing."

"Armoring the spear tip," I say slowly, wondering what the hell they are talking about. "I need workable metal for that. What do you think I am doing?"

Dallas shrugs. "Taking your frustrations out on that poor can."

It's a strange moment. I am weak. My brain sluggish. And feeling this disconnected from both of them is very uncomfortable.

"You got a better way?" I ask.

She shakes her head and I turn away and ignore them. There are three of us now and that means that any social conflicts will be uneven. June has pulled away from me so naturally her and Dallas are feeling closer.

I understand it, but I don't like it.

Once there is one break in the can, the rest is easy and I can flip one of the quarters back and forth until that seam breaks. I lay the piece of metal, which is a quarter of the can, against the newly sharpened point of the first spear, take one of the small one-pound green propane bottles for the stove, and start beating the metal into shape, wrapping it around the spear tip.

It's awkward and slow. The propane bottle isn't easy to grip, but it's metal and the best hammer I can think of.

I beat the metal into place so that it awkwardly wraps part of the spear tip. Something is tickling in my brain as I do it, but I can't bring it forth. Some idea that would make this all easier.

I shrug it off. June and Dallas are whispering behind me, but I shrug that off too. I beat the metal around the wood. Slowly. Carefully. There are gaps but it's not bad. The metal will reinforce the spear tip considerably if it stays on. But how?

I remove the metal which is bent into a rough spiral and consider it. If I can bend some of the edges tightly, I can drive them into the wood.

More whispers.

If I was feeling normal, I would have been fine, but I'm barely able to do this, my hands hurting from using them and they are making me clumsy, my head is light. "Something you two want to share?" I ask.

Dallas smiles sweetly. "No, Woody, we just like to watch you work."

And then jealousy flares up in me. Dallas wants June, she's over there reinforcing the division between us so she can have June for herself.

I feel shame at the thought. Thinking that Dallas would do that. Thinking that June is mine in some way. Feeling like she is something I need to protect from others.

I almost say something stupid. I almost let the jealousy out. But this is my family. We have our disagreements and fights, but not over something like this. I can't let that happen even if June does end up with Dallas.

I sigh, doing my best to let it all go. The fatigue of my recovery is lying thick on me. "I need to get this to stay on," I say, illustrating how the metal slides on and off the spear tip. "Any ideas?"

Survival first. Romantic relationships second.

June looks around on the floor of the treehouse and pulls up a rusted nail, one that came out when they pried the second one-by-one loose. "Nail?" she asks.

"Perfect," I say. "Can you help me?"

Her face lights up with a smile and I feel silly for all the paranoid jealousy. She slides over and together we nail the metal in place. It takes a while, it's really dorky, it won't hold forever, but it should work better.

I feel better with June next to me. I resolve to let that be enough. If we can't be a couple, we can still be partners in the crazy apocalypse.

"Thank you," I say with a smile when it's done.

She nods and smiles back.

"Dallas and I will work on the second spear while you're down there," I say. "Hopefully, this is an improvement."

I have hope for survival. I have hope for June and I being, at the very least, companions.

Beyond that, I shoo away all the sparks of hope and the despair that can come with them and focus on one small thing at a time.

CHAPTER SEVEN

WITH DALLAS'S HELP, the next spear tip is better. Two heads are better than one, especially with the shape my head is in. We fold one of the quarters of a tin can in half, stick the spear in it, and pound it around the point. It ends up looking more like an arrowhead with the excess metal flaring out. We then pound the flares down and drive a single nail through it.

That's the hard part, getting the nail to pierce the metal of the can.

Half an hour later, June is back, flushed and sweating but with a smile on her face. "Forty more," she says.

I get up and hand her a bottle of water and take the spear, the metal tip is gone and the wooden point dull again. She takes the water bottle and our fingers touch, but the connection doesn't linger. She drinks and sits and stares at me.

"You're pale," she says. "You need to rest."

I nod. "I will. As soon as we get the system worked out."

She bites her lip and keeps staring at me. I get the distinct impression it is nurse June staring at me not girlfriend June.

She rests for a few minutes and then digs in her backpack and pulls out a red bandana and ties it tightly around her nose and mouth before taking the improved spear and clanging her way back down the ladder.

"You okay?" Dallas asks. She's whittling away at the spear and I'm staring where June just was.

I shrug.

"Thought we were best friends," Dallas says, and it's not lost on me that she has a sharp knife in her hand. "Least that's what you told me before we went to Flagstaff and risked our lives multiple times to rescue your girl there from Talia and Phantom Company."

I look at her, her eyes narrow, her whittling stops.

"What?" I ask.

"Best friends talk," she says. "Since we got June back, you and me, we don't talk that much."

Shit. I don't want these relationship compilations.

"I'm sorry," I say. "You are right. Best friends talk." I've got another quarter of a can in my hands and am trying to figure out how to optimize the process.

"So talk, Woody," Dallas says.

"We need to do this," I say, gesturing with the can down below where June is spearing Zs.

She snorts. "It's not like we can't talk and pound on cans at the same time."

I look into her brown eyes. "I feel like shit, Dallas. Even doing this is stupidly hard. What do you want from me?"

"I want you to be my friend, Woody," she says, swallowing hard, and it hits me. Winslow screwed us all up. Dallas being chained to the statue and so vulnerable. Me almost dying. June having to do something really stupid to save me.

I take a deep breath and nod. I'm not the only one struggling here. "Do you want to talk about Winslow?" I ask, sipping some water.

She nods shyly. "It was bad," she says.

"I would have, you know," I say, handing her the water. Neither of us have been drinking enough.

"You would have what?" she asks.

"If it came down to it," I begin with a shrug. "I wouldn't have let you become a Z. I would have done what was necessary. I would have hated myself, but I would have done it."

Dallas stares at me blinking, the water bottle at her lips. She had begged me there on the corner in Winslow chained to the statue of Glenn Frey with the zombie horde closing in on us to kill her. I had avoided giving her a direct answer. I didn't want to admit how bad the situation was.

She lowers the water bottle. "When you were sick up here, when we didn't know if you would make it..." She trails off and licks her lips. "I told June I would take care of it if you... you know. I wouldn't ask that of her."

Of course they had discussed that as June tended to me for three days. It only makes sense. And I realize that June and Dallas had three days to talk, to get to know each other better, to share what they needed to share since we rescued June from the bottom of the Grand Canyon at Phantom Ranch.

"Thank you," I say, and then she is hugging me. We're both sitting so it's a little awkward, but she hugs me hard and I hug her back. Dallas has her sarcastic, acerbic exterior, but she's just hiding her vulnerability.

"Is June..." I whisper. "Are June and I... Do you know anything?"

She lets me go and her eyes are kind. "Just give her a little space, okay? And, you know, try talking to her."

I nod and pick the metal from the can back up. "We need a better way to attach this. The nails are too hard."

Dallas smiles and nods. I know we are not done talking, that we need to keep talking, that I need to talk. There's too much going on here to hold it in. But survival is first, and together we get to work on improving the spear tip.

CHAPTER EIGHT

THIS IS OUR DAY. June working like a fiend stabbing zombies in the head with our jury-rigged spears. Dallas and I talking and working on the spears. I get a few short naps in, but we are all needed for this operation.

We end up with a better system for armoring the spear. We use one quarter of a can folded in half, but then we poke some holes in it with a knife and bend the metal. When we pound the metal onto the stick and the metal bites into the wood, it holds it reasonably well without a nail.

We also stop sharpening the sticks so much and let the metal be the sharp point. It's crude but it lasts long enough for a session.

June also gets into a rhythm. Half an hour down with the bandana over her mouth to deal with the stench while she takes out about forty Zs. Another half an hour for climbing up and down the ladder and rest. Her pace has slowed, not because of the spear but because of fatigue. She switches arms regularly, but it's very hard work.

After five hours of this she's pretty wiped out, and about 250 of about 4,000 Zs are down. That's better than my thirty-an-hour pace when I did the math, but it is not looking sustainable.

When June flops down, clearly exhausted, Dallas says, "My turn."

"What about your ankle?" I ask.

She shrugs. "I can climb the damn ladder with one good leg, it just won't be fast."

June nods and I can see the relief on her face. "Stay above the reach of their arms," she says. "And that's higher than you think, the bodies are starting to stack up down there."

June takes off the makeshift harness and hands it to her. Dallas ties a bandana over her nose, puts on the harness, and goes over the edge. Right before her face disappears, she catches my eye and nods at June.

I nod back. My stomach is rioting at the thought of it, but I know we need to talk.

"Are you okay?" I ask after Dallas has disappeared and we can hear the slow clang of her hopping down the ladder.

"Just tired," she says, rolling her shoulders and flexing her hands. She leans in, looking closely at me. "You're pale, Woody. You need to sleep."

I shrug. "I need to keep these spears going for you."

I get to work and she's silent, but I can feel her gaze on me.

It's a one-person operation now that we've got it worked out and it only takes about fifteen minutes. Whittle the wood down. Fold and poke holes in the metal. Pound it on carefully with the propane bottle and make sure the bent bits of metal have a good grip, and then fold over the extra flanges.

And then there is nothing to do. June is sitting quietly and I realize that she was watching me the whole time.

I smile but it feels twisted on my face. I'd rather face down a dozen Zs with just a baseball bat than start this conversation. Relationships change, and I know ours has, but I don't know *how* it has. Because of the life and death nature of our days, the apocalypse has driven us quickly past the giddy passions of early love. Opening my mouth here could leave me with June being no more than a friend.

And, yeah, I know I've said that would be fine. That I will take any and all the June I can get. And that is true, and at the same time I want so much more.

I need more.

And this is not the time or place to need someone as much as I need her.

"So... um... Winslow," I stammer after the spear is done and set aside.

She just stares at me, her face passive and unreadable. June is not one of those people that speak their every emotion as soon as they feel them, so it's often hard to tell where her head is at.

I remember what Dallas said, "Just give her a little space, okay? And, you know, try talking to her." Am I doing that? This is talking to her, but I don't know if it's giving her space.

"I didn't know if..." I continue, clearly having trouble with the English language. "And then you.... And then I..." I end up holding out my scratched hands. The zombie scratches are scabbed up and bleeding in a few spots from all that I've been doing with my hands.

She's still staring at me, but her lips are pursed and she's blinking.

"And since I woke up," I continue, unable to stop now, "you've been... I'm not complaining, I am grateful that you saved my life. I... I just don't know where we are at."

She's silent for a long time and shouts float up with the snarling of the Zs. Joyous curses, actually, as Dallas celebrates her kills with colorful language. It sounds like she's having fun.

"When I was at Phantom Ranch," June begins, "when I didn't think I'd ever see you again. I..." She looks away and sighs. "I mean, I knew you would try to rescue me, and I figured you'd die trying, but I had no idea what you were going through."

She looks at me, her ocean-blue eyes so sad. I want to do nothing more than touch her, than to hold her, but I give her the space Dallas urged me to give her.

She bites her lip, takes a breath, and goes on. "And then we lost

Dallas and that felt... terrible. And then the horde surrounded you and..." She gets up and walks to the other side of the treehouse and stares out over the high desert.

It's early afternoon and the day has turned hot, around eighty degrees, the sky blue, but the washed-out blue of the desert, not the startling blue of the mountains. She staring to the south to the snaking greenery of the Little Colorado River.

I lever myself up and use the spear as a walking stick and stand next to her.

"I had no idea what you must have gone through," she says quietly. "Trying to get me back. Knowing that the odds were terrible but fighting for all you were worth. Risking your life repeatedly." She takes a deep breath. "I had no idea."

"It wasn't easy," I say, quietly. "I had lost what I cared about most in this world and didn't want to be in this world without it."

Yeah. That phrasing is a little awkward, but I was still trying to give her a little space, not whack her with a grand romantic gesture.

"I understand what that feels like now," she says.

I'm staring at her lovely face, but she's still looking towards the south.

The little sparks of hope are flaring, begging for my attention, but I ignore them. I just breathe. I take in the beauty of the woman I love. I try not to project where this conversation will go or what state our relationship will be in.

I turn away and look to the south too and let there be silence between us. A good relationship has to have room for silence. We are stuck up here, there will be more time to talk, more time to sort through all of this.

"Hot damn!" Dallas says as she clangs up the ladder and steps into the treehouse. "Now that was fun! Hard as hell, but fun."

June turns to me and our eyes briefly meet. There is sadness there and a fierce determination. She takes the spear from me and our hands touch and she lets her fingers linger there for just a moment.

So many sparks of hope, but I let them all go.

June turns to Dallas and asks, "How was it?"

I watch as they chatter, as Dallas shucks the harness and June puts it on. As Dallas hands me the blunted and armor-less spear.

After June has disappeared, Dallas walks up to me, punches me in the shoulder—not the one with the bullet wound, thank God—and says, "Who's your best friend now? Hope you made good use of your time."

CHAPTER NINE

THIS IS how our team works now, the Woody, June, and Dallas Post-Apocalyptic Survival Trio. June and Dallas are the warriors taking turns with the Zs, and I am the master of arms, whittling and armoring the spears.

June and I don't talk about anything serious, both girls taking cat naps between rounds, and I do too once the spear is ready.

With them alternating, they are able to sustain the pace. We end the day at sundown with about ten hours of zombie spearing in and about five hundred Zs down.

It's a disgusting mess down there, even from up here I can see it, a rising mound of no longer undead zombie flesh that the Zs have to climb up on to try to reach us.

The press of their numbers still makes that possible, but the sheer mass of rotting flesh is becoming worrisome on several levels.

Rotting flesh, for one. And rotting more than when the fungus-heads were "alive." That just can't be a healthy thing to be around.

How high the pile will get, for another. And how we'll actually navigate through the piled remains of four thousand Zs to walk out of here.

Or what about when there are thousands of them quickly rotting below us, all the flies of Northern Arizona feasting on them? Will we even be able to survive the stench, and what kind of a toxic environment is that?

And while we can get four spear tips out of a can, we will be burning through five a day, won't we run out? And I have to whittle the spears down a little every time, and they are slowly getting shorter.

But I keep that all to myself as Dallas serves a quick stew she made out of some of the canned goods stashed here. We need the cans and the stew is a bizarre combination of clam chowder soup, peas, corn, and garbanzo beans, but after what I've been through it's a feast.

June gives me the clear to eat a little of it and see how it goes. I've been keeping food down and I want to wolf it, but restrain myself.

There was only one bowl up here and Dallas gives me that while they eat out of empty cans that will be spear tips tomorrow.

"To killing us some Zs," Dallas says, raising her can in toast. I clink my blue plastic bowl against their cans. Dallas's face squeezes as she raises the can and puts it down and rubs her shoulders. "God, am I sore."

I watch June and her chat about the day's labor and complain about their sore muscles and wonder how they can possibly keep it up.

It's dark out and we've got a small light going, one of my solar chargers that has an LED light built in. It casts a ghostly glow on their faces. The desert cools quickly so they are back in their jackets and I've got a sleeping bag around my shoulders.

For a moment, it seems normal. The strange smell of the food mostly drives away the scent of the Zs and their chatting covers up most of the sound of them below.

It's almost like we are camping and the zombie apocalypse is just a story told around campfires to elicit scared giggles, not a swarming reality below us.

I take a deep breath and close my eyes and let it out in a slow sigh. This is what counts. This right here. Three friends, having survived the day. There hasn't been laughter, Dallas's frenzied whooping as she slayed Zs the closest thing, but this is enough for today.

There hasn't been any resolution between June and me, but we did talk. She does care or else she wouldn't be feeling all that she is.

"...when we've gotten every last one of them?" Dallas is asking, but I missed the first part in my reverie. "Earth to Woody," Dallas says in a deep voice. "Come in, Woody."

"What?" I ask, shaking it off.

"I asked," Dallas says, "where will we go when we've split all the heads there are to split below?"

I'm taken aback. My moment of normalcy shattered, the scent and smell of the Zs floating up and my stomach is no longer so happy with Dallas's strange stew.

"Umm... I..." I stammer, trying to get my head into gear. "Joseph City is a few miles to the east. There's a coal power plant there, you can just see the two stacks sticking up from here. I guess we would go there and see if we can find some transportation."

Dallas nods. "I remember it. I was with Talia's group after they 'recruited' me in Holbrook as we came west. The plant is creepy as hell."

"Did you guys trap the Zs there like in Winslow?" June asks.

Dallas shakes her head, the low light making her face look eerie. "Too small. We drove through fast, only a few encounters with Zs."

"So we'll be on foot going into a small town fully populated with Zs?" June asks Dallas, but then turns and looks at me.

"We can't go back to Winslow," I say. "From Joseph City we can head north up to the rez or south down towards the White Mountains. Or we could keep going east to Holbrook, but I think that's a bad idea."

"What will Talia be expecting?" Dallas asks.

"One of those," I say with a shrug. "It's the logical thing to do so that's what she will expect."

"And plan for?" June asks.

I shrug again. "If what she said in the video is true, if she does have business to attend to, we just have to get out of here in time. If that was a lie then, yes, she gave us the means to escape and will have something waiting for us."

"So let's go back to Winslow," June says, her tone flat and even. She's staring at me.

"Winslow!" Dallas says. "Have you lost your freaking mind?"

"Hear me out," June says. "I think Woody is right, that Talia overextended with us and she must have some internal conflicts to deal with or another Flagstaff gang. I also think she thought through our escape and our likely paths away from here. She probably left enough personnel out here to resume her damn game when we get out of here."

I nod. She's right. Talia hasn't anticipated everything we've done but enough to keep her twisted game going. "So Winslow is where she won't expect," I say.

June smiles at me and my heart beats a little faster. "And there won't be Zs," she says. "After we get down, if Dallas's ankle is healed enough, we head out on foot. No roads. We walk at night and hide during the day. Let her search where it is logical to go. Let's do something less logical. A lot less logical."

The silence is thick after she's done, except for the snarling Zs, of course, but their prospective meals aren't close so they aren't that loud.

"After Winslow?" Dallas finally asks.

June bites her lip, her eyes darting between the two of us. "After Winslow," she says slowly, "we go back to the Grand Canyon and the Phantom Ranch. Like we all decided at Meteor Crater before this stupid game of Talia's started. She will be going back there for them. We get there before her. We help them defend themselves. We make a stand."

She pauses and licks her lips and stares at each of us for a moment or two and says, "If you two are still up for it."

I'm stunned. While I was sick and recovering, while I was worrying about the state of our relationship, June was thinking it all through. It's a desperate plan, we'll have to be smart, but it makes sense. Phantom Ranch is a great place to survive the apocalypse with the Colorado River right there and a long growing season, but their security sucked and they weren't using tech at all. We could help them a lot.

"I'm in," I say.

We are both staring at Dallas and she slowly nods. "Let's go ruin that bitch's life."

We laugh, all of us. It's the strained laughter of three survivors with a crazy plan that has little chance of succeeding. But it's laughter, hitting my second rule for each post-apocalyptic day. And we survived, so that takes care of rule one. And I spent the day with June and that's rule three. This officially makes it a good day.

We eat and chat about crazy plans until the food is done and our exhaustion takes us.

CHAPTER TEN

"YOU AWAKE?" June whispers, her voice so low I can barely hear it above the low growls of the Zs below us, still complaining that they haven't made a meal of us yet.

"Yeah," I whisper back, sitting slowly up. "Is everything okay?"

She nods. The crescent moon is up and she is a grey shadow in front of me. "It's cold," she says. "Can I join you? Just for warmth."

We only have two sleeping bags because Talia only expected two of us to make it here.

"It's all I have to give," I say. I am feeling stronger but still quite weak.

I unzip the bag a ways and she slides in next to me and I zip it back up around us both. She is pressed against me, I can smell her sweat and that strange June sweetness that I always smell when she is close. I wish I was feeling better and that our relationship was clear.

She is shivering, so I put my arms around her and pull her close. She holds me back and it is good.

I think I have held an unrealistic view of June in my mind. I used to think the only thing in the world she is afraid of is Talia. After all, in Albuquerque she faked her death via zombie just to escape Talia.

It was just a freak chance that brought us all back together in the Grand Canyon.

But June is human and humans feel fear. Especially now. Tons of it. June just doesn't show her fear very much, being the trained warrior that she is. But after our talk earlier, it's clear that she's afraid of losing me and that is probably what this distance is about.

At least some of the distance.

As I hold her, as her shivering slows, I don't say anything like that. Just because we are physically close doesn't mean I can't give her the space Dallas told me she needs.

"Why are you awake?" she whispers when the shivers leave her.

"Thinking about your plan," I say.

"It's *our* plan now." I can hear some amusement in her hushed voice.

And it is our plan. I agreed to this madness.

"Any brilliant insights?" she asks.

"Well... beyond it being mad and us having little chance of success?" I ask.

She jabs me in the ribs and says, "Yes. Beyond that."

"We are not going fast enough," I say. The silvery glow of the moon is giving me just enough light to see the contours of her round face, but I can't see her expression.

"Killing the Zs?" she asks.

"Yes," I say. "Talia gave us two weeks' rations, told us that would be long enough for her to deal with her thing. There's no way she's leaving us for that long. She was planting a number in our heads of an amount of time she has no intention of letting us have."

"She might not make it," June whispers, but there is no conviction in her voice. "We might not see her again."

"And we can't plan for that," I say. "We have to go faster."

"How?" she asks.

"She only expected two of us to survive," I say. "If we all three are slaying Zs it will go faster."

She doesn't reply right away and I was expecting a quick no. She takes a few breaths and gives me a squeeze. "Okay, but you'll have to start out slow and rest a lot."

"Right," I say.

"You better get some sleep then," she says, ending the conversation.

I am awake for a while, feeling June close and wanting more. Worrying about Talia and her plans and if we can actually escape from here.

OUR SECOND DAY spearing zombies is a grind. Unrelenting. Difficult. Disgusting.

We have a quick breakfast before the sun is up and June scurries down with a spear as soon as there is enough light to see.

June does a half hour down, then Dallas, and then I go down for my first shift with the spear.

I have no coat and it is still cold but I have on every shirt I own, which is just a T-shirt, a long-sleeve T, and a flannel shirt. It's a lumpy mass that makes it a little hard to move, but it's a small thing in the scheme of things.

The Zs are amassed around the ladder when I get down, their grubby hands reaching up to me. In the dim, early light they look almost black and white, this sea of need and longing.

They are up about two or three feet higher than they should be, the mass of the recently speared Zs grinding under their feet. They are relentless hunger and need. They are the worst impulses of humanity. And they smell badly enough, all rotting meat and moldy flesh, so that I have to swallow hard not to retch right then and there despite the bandana over my nose.

I stop a rung above their grasping hands and clip myself and the spear onto the ladder. I am a little dizzy and still feel weak, but I am much better than when I woke up two days ago.

The hands are a waving distraction making these thousands of Zs seem like a single entity. There are heads, but the hands and the arms are all in the way.

I get a good grip on the spear, towards the end of it. I've got work gloves on for the cold and for my grip. I thrust down and hear the sharp sound of a skull cracking. The Z goes down and is quickly replaced like it was never there.

This really is that Greek myth about the guy rolling the rock up the hill but he can't push it all the way over, his strength fails, the stone rolls back down the hill, and he has to do it over again. Forever.

I think that's the gist of the myth—whatever it is, I can't look it up.

My second stab skitters off the greasy hair of a woman Z and my next one gets her in the shoulder. My fourth is true and she disappears under the sea of unrelenting need.

I stop counting stabs of the spear and start counting Zs down. One. Two. Three. Four. My body is warming up with the exercise, my arm feeling the strain of wielding the spear. It feels good to move, to breathe, but the air is so bad I am not breathing as deeply as I should.

Five. Six. Seven. It takes several stabs on average to get one in the head, always having to spear through the ocean of hands and arms like it's some kind of living sea creature.

Eight. Nine. Ten. I take a moment, trying to suck in air through the bandana that isn't so fetid and switch hands. My eyes are watering from the fumes and I can taste the moldy smell it is so intense.

Eleven. Twelve. Thirteen. It all begins to blur together. I'm not sure if the last one I got was male or female, young or old. They are all the same, all one expression of desperate need.

Fourteen. Fifteen. Sixteen. It's starting to feel like this is all I have ever done. Stood on this metal ladder, holding on with one hand, stabbing down with our makeshift spear with the other, longing to hear the sharp crack of the skull bone breaking.

Seventeen. Eighteen. Nineteen. I stab down harder, letting my sudden anger fuel me. They are all Talias, a sea of undead Talias with her blond hair darkened by grime, her tall wiry body easy to see in the more emaciated Zs.

Twenty. Twenty-one. Twenty-two. I quickly switch hands and kill Talia again and again. She may not be a Z, but her need is like theirs, her desperation is like theirs. She is constantly grasping for us, constantly trying to capture us, to consume us.

Twenty-tree. Twenty-four. Twenty-five. I thought I heard something, but I don't care. I'm stabbing down harder and quicker at all the Talias. I'm getting my revenge. Nothing else matters. Not the stench. Not my watering eyes. Not my fatiguing body. Not my increasing dizziness.

"Woody!" June shouts from just above me, finally breaking through my fugue.

I stop, panting hoarsely, and look up. There is concern written on her face. I stare, blinking, still feeling the rage, and wonder if this is what has been fueling June and Dallas down here.

"What happened?" she asks. "Your fifteen minutes are up. Time for a break."

"They all started looking like Talia," I say with a shrug. "I couldn't stop."

She gives me a grim smile and a small nod. Maybe she does understand. "Well, I hope you feel better then. Let's go."

I look back just to reassure myself that they are not all Talia and follow June up the ladder.

THIS IS OUR DAY. From before sunrise until after sunset. We rotate through, all of us taking our turns down below with the Zs, resharpening and armoring the spears, resting as best we can. Over twelve hours we do it, as long as there is enough light.

My shifts are about fifteen minutes and June and Dallas each do about thirty minutes. It drives us each to the brink of exhaustion, and our dinner stew made from random canned goods is a quiet affair, the groans of us sore living mingling with the snarls of the dead-ish below us.

I say "dead-ish" because they really aren't un-dead. The fungus animates their bodies, provides them with senses and desires. Dead-ish characterizes it best. Because they aren't alive in the normal sense, but they aren't really dead.

"Final count?" June asks Dallas between lethargic bites. Dallas volunteered to do the tally.

She wipes her mouth and looks at some plywood she's been scratching on, leaning in close in the dim LED light. "Seven hundred and two," she says. "Rough total from yesterday was five hundred, bringing our grand total to twelve-hundred and two. Approximately."

"Five more days at this pace," June says, her gaze turning to me. "Think you can keep it up?"

I feel the sting of her question, but it's fair given how sick I was. I flex my hands slowly, the scratches bled some today because of how much I used my hands. I am sore. I am exhausted. But those feelings are just normal soreness and exhaustion. "Yeah. I think so, but..."

"But what?" Dallas asks.

June nods at me and turns to Dallas. "We chatted last night when you were snoring up a storm."

"I do not snore," Dallas says.

"Oh yes you do," June says, a smile on her face.

Dallas wasn't snoring when June and I were talking, but I did hear her snore a little during the night. Nothing serious and something I've been living with as long as Dallas and I have been sleeping in the same proximity.

But I don't say anything. I just eat my stew and watch.

I expect a fight from Dallas, for her to rise to the bait, for a moment or two of entertainment. But that is not what happens. "Forget about whether I do or do not snore," she says. "What did you guys talk about? I thought we were doing good. We need to keep this up for five more days and we'll be in the clear. What was that 'but' about?"

"There's no buts about your snoring," June says.

"What did you guys talk about?" Dallas asks with a sigh.

June sighs too, clearly not getting what she was looking for from Dallas and nods at me.

I tell Dallas what I told June last night and watch as Dallas starts to chew on her lower lip. "There is no way we have as much time as Talia led us to believe we had," I say, summing it up. "And with us as tired as we all are right now, I don't see how we keep this pace up and have anything left to escape with."

It's quiet, except for the snarling below us, as everyone thinks about it. After the exhausting activity of the day, it's a sobering thought and I don't have the energy for coming up with a good idea.

"What about the dynamite?" Dallas asks after the silence has gone on for a while. "There are less of them now."

I shake my head. "It just won't get that many of them."

"Can't you do something to make it more deadly?" Dallas asks. "More effective? Like the nails you glued to dynamite of your suicide vest?"

I appreciate the effort but I am having trouble thinking straight. "Nails will make it more deadly, but it's still one stick. We need more oomph."

We sit there for a while longer, our food forgotten and my brain in neutral.

"We'll talk about this again tomorrow," June says. "Eat up, we need all the sleep we can get."

CHAPTER ELEVEN

DAY three of our mission to slay four thousand Zs with a spear starts out before the sun is up with the three of us moving slower than the zombies below.

We're beat to hell from what we've been through, all of us sporting various kinds of injuries. We're undernourished and sore as hell from the slaying already done. We're exhausted and the thought of five more days of this is demoralizing. But we eat, more canned goods surprise stew, and June goes down the ladder first in the thinnest of predawn light.

"Five more days," Dallas groans as she shovels in the last of her food and swallows. It doesn't look like she's tasting it at all. In the dim, light her pink down jacket looks less pink, which is good. It's way too early and I'm way too tired for something like that.

"At least," I say. The sleep didn't do anything to help my pessimism. June was in the sleeping bag with me all night, but it was strictly platonic. We need to talk more, but I lack the energy and I have to save every bit of my will to deal with the Zs. At least the sleeping bag wrapped around me reminds me of her closeness. I missed having her close, even platonically.

"This is what she wanted?" Dallas asks.

It takes me a moment to translate "she" into "Talia," my brain is so sluggish. I nod. "Yes. This is the kind of shape she wants us in when she returns and her stupid game moves on to its next challenge."

"I hate her," Dallas says without any energy.

"I started pretending all the Zs are her," I say. "It helps... a little."

Dallas snorts but doesn't quite laugh. Probably as close as we're going to get today to laughter. "So you're saying that Talia is going to sweep in, right around the time we are done with the Zs and exhausted and too sore to move, and shove us into her next challenge?"

"Yes," I say, taking another bite of food. This batch has a can of chili in it and I think creamed corn. It's kind of gross but it's calories, and any calories in an apocalypse. "We are all still alive so the game can't be over yet."

Dallas stabs her spork angrily into the can she is using to eat out of, the clinking sound of it sharp and loud. She sighs and says, "I guess we better get the second spear armored."

I nod but don't move. The morning is cold and I still don't have a jacket so I am reluctant to leave the warmth of the sleeping bag.

Dallas gets up, limps over to the other side of our treehouse home, and rummages in the built-in storage boxes. Her ankle is getting better despite all the activity. She has a pronounced limp but at least she can walk some now. She comes back with an empty can from last night, the food remnants dried on the inside, and a green one-pound propane tank.

She sits down right next to me, pulls the multi-tool from her belt, flips open the can opener tool, and starts in on the unopened side of the can.

It's slow going, but everything about this is slow going. She looks up after a while, nods at the propane tank which is dinged and scarred from us using it as a hammer, and says, "I've been wondering. We are using that as a hammer and it's full of compressed flammable gasses. Why haven't we blown ourselves up?"

"The tank is strong," I say, "it can take a little pounding."

She nods and keeps working with the can opener, the groaning of metal joining the louder sound of the Zs now that June is closer to them.

Something tickles in my tired brain. Yesterday Dallas asked how we could make the dynamite more effective. Today she asked why we weren't blowing ourselves up by using the propane tanks as hammers. Something had tickled my tired brain when I first grabbed one of the tanks to hammer with, but it didn't come through until now.

"Dallas! You are brilliant," I say, leaning over and pulling her into a big hug.

"Well. Yeah, of course I am," she says as I squeeze her. "What did I do this time?"

I let her go, walk over to the ladder, and yell down. "June! I've got a plan! Get up here."

CHAPTER TWELVE

THEY'RE both looking at me like this better be good. June's back up from spearing Zs and Dallas is pissed because I wouldn't say anything before June got here. They are both impatient and it shows, their arms crossed as we sit in a triangle on the hard wood in the middle of the cell tower treehouse.

The light is still thin but plenty to see the frown on June's face. This battle may be exhausting, but she is much better suited to it than I am. Something about it feeds her, and it just wears me out. I know, I'm still recovering from the zombie infection, but there is something different about how she meets these kinds of challenges.

"It's going to take some prep," I say with a grin. "But I think we can blow most of them up. The risk to us is not insignificant, but I believe that can be managed."

I wait for the cries of joy, the begging for details, but they both just keep staring at me. And I guess I get it. I had said, multiple times, that the one stick dynamite was not enough.

"You can thank Dallas," I say to June.

"Me?" Dallas asks.

"Yes, you." I pick up the propane tank we have been using as a hammer. "One stick of dynamite is not enough, but if we use all the propane tanks we have. Then..."

"Boom...?" June asks.

I nod. "The dynamite will breach the tanks, and as the propane expands, as enough oxygen mixes in... then boom."

"How much of a boom?" Dallas asks.

I shrug. "I'm not a demolitions expert and I've never done this before, but it should work. The tanks will also turn into shrapnel which will do more damage."

"What about the risk?" June asks.

"The flying shrapnel could make it up this far," I say, "and it's possible that the blast could weaken the tower."

"Those are some damn risks," Dallas says.

"And managing those risks?" June asks. Her demeanor has changed. She's no longer agitated but leaning forward and engaged, her voice eager.

"I don't think half an inch of plywood is enough to protect us from the shrapnel," I say, banging the wood we are sitting on. "We need to deconstruct it so we have three layers or so to sit on during the explosion."

June smiles and nods, but Dallas bites her lip and asks, "What about the danger to the tower?"

I shrug. "We'll drop it down into the center of the tower, into the center of the horde, but otherwise we are taking our chances."

"Odds?" June asks.

"Of the tower falling?" I ask, and she nods. "It would be a wild guess."

"So guess," she says.

I get up and walk over to the edge and bang on one of the corner poles of the tower. It rings hollowly. "This thing is about eight inches in diameter, hollow, maybe half an inch thick. Steel. I strap the dynamite directly to it, it might take it out, but just one of many. On the ground in the center of the tower it should be fine. The shrapnel could damage it, but it shouldn't break it."

"Give us a number," Dallas says.

I shrug again because It's a wild guess. "I'd say 1 or 2 percent chance of the tower being badly damaged, less than that for it actually coming down."

I walk back to them, the creaking of the wood under my feet more noticeable now that I'm thinking about explosions and shrapnel. I sit down. "We would need today to prep and we could blow them up in the morning."

"And then we head back to the Canyon?" June asks. Is she looking for a quid-pro-quo here? She will support my plan if I support hers. What is going on with her? I already backed her plan.

"Works for me," I say.

"And you think we'll be out of here before Talia is back?" Dallas asks. "That she didn't expect this?"

"She didn't think we'd have dynamite in Winslow," June says.

"And that's one of the reasons she blew up our truck," I say. "She thought she was eliminating the rest."

"But what if she accounted for this?" Dallas asks, looking around.

And I get it. We should be paranoid about Talia. We have good reason. But she can't anticipate everything.

I'm at a loss for words, but June isn't. "Then we are less exhausted than we would be if we had speared every one of them," she says. "Then we have something left for her stupid game."

Dallas takes a deep breath and lets out a long sigh. "Okay. Let's blow them snarlers up."

CHAPTER THIRTEEN

PREPARING to blow up three thousand Zs is exhausting. Not in the monotonous way of trying to spear them one at a time, but it still is. By the time the sun is all the way up, we are all at work on the tree-house taking it apart.

It is a triangular structure about twelve feet across made up of a hodgepodge of wood and metal signs that are nailed, screwed, and tied together with walls about three feet high on all sides except for a gap where the ladder of the cell tower is.

And we have no hammers, only multi-tools and knives. Nothing like taking on a job with the wrong tools.

We start on the sides first, using multi-tools for the screws when we are lucky, cutting string and zip ties when we are very lucky, and when we are unlucky and it's nails, we have to resort to using our knives and kicking the board to loosen them, and then using the spears as leverage when there is enough room.

The construction of this is something of a marvel. Despite the hodgepodge nature of it, it is a strong, stable structure that took time and an enormous amount of energy to build. Sure it creaks. Sure some of the boards are sistered together and that makes me pretty nervous when I finally see the underside of it, but the treehouse is solid.

This took time to build. Talia and her people didn't do this, others did. That's clear to me now. It had to be more than one person. I'd say at least three or four to scrounge the wood, haul it up, and find ways to attach it all.

Who were they? Where did they go?

Of particular interest to me is how they attached the supporting joists, mostly two-by-six pieces of lumber, to the tower. As we work, I keep looking at it. Maybe distracting myself, maybe storing it away for future use.

The cell tower has three main poles, those eight-inch pipes that form a triangle on the ground and taper as the cell tower rises. Joining them are smaller pipes that form squashed Xs as they flow up the tower joining the three central pipes.

The joists of the treehouse, often made up of multiple two-by-sixes and some two-by-fours sistered together, are too long and stick out, resting where the X supports join the main pipe and bound together with thick cord.

Simple and strong. At first, I feel sad for the builders, thinking they didn't make it, but then I decide since this is just a story I'm making up, that I should make up a better one. So I decide that they heard of a better place to survive and left this desolate desert by choice.

There's plenty that's smart about this treehouse. You are safe from Zs. You can see danger coming. You can sleep soundly. Makes me imagine a future where there are cell tower treehouses all over the place for travelers, kind of like post-apocalyptic hostels.

My ruminations don't slow me down though. We work slowly and carefully—we are about fifty feet off the ground after all.

The goal is for at least an inch of wood and some metal between us and the potential shrapnel. That means if we take off all the sides, lay them down on top of each other, we can do better than that. The hodgepodge nature of the construction means that some boards are eight feet long, but many are not. We've got two stop signs, a couple of "one way" signs, and a faded green sign with white lettering that says "Winslow" and points to the right.

"That goes on top," I say after Dallas pulls it down. The back side had been facing us and I hadn't realized what it said.

"Sure thing, boss," Dallas says. "I'm happy for Winslow to kiss my sweet ass."

With the wood and the signs, we should end up with six or seven layers we can stack up and all three of us can fit on. Some of the wood used on the sides is thinner than the floor, but we'll have about two inches of wood and some metal below us when the explosion happens.

It's hard work, the late spring day getting warm and the wrong tools for the job slowing us down, but I notice a lightening in all of our moods, the soreness and the fatigue, if not forgotten, then less heavy. There's cursing and frustration because this would be easy with the right tools, but it's almost like we're having fun.

It's those sparks of hope buzzing around and I let them in this time, but only a little. Limited hope seems to be the only sane hope in this post-apocalyptic world. I have hope that this will take out most of the rest of the Zs. I have hope that we will survive the day. I even have hope that there will be some laughter today.

And this is not idle hope. This is hope we are actively pushing for. We are not wishing for the future we want, we are trying to create it, and that seems like an inherently hopeful thing.

"Winslow's going to be nice when we're done," Dallas says as we are taking a break, a couple boards removed but nails still left to bang out. We are going to save all the nails for our little bomb. "No Zs," she continues, "someone's going to hole up there."

"Talia," June says, a sour look on her face. She takes a sip from a water bottle and passes it to me.

"Of course," Dallas says. "That bitch never does something with only one purpose. She was using us to lure the Zs away from

Winslow. She's using us to destroy them. She's going to take up resi-
dence there."

"Shit," I say, invoking the official word of the apocalypse. I hadn't
seen it, but they are right. "Winters aren't nearly as bad as Flagstaff,"
I say. "The Little Colorado is there, and while it doesn't run year-
round, it is a source of water."

"So she must have left people there," June says. She's still looking
towards the next steps of our journey.

I am desperate to talk to her. I'm feeling better than when we last
talked and think I might do a decent job of it now, but this is not the
time. Maybe tonight. "So we have to avoid Winslow," I say.

She nods. "And Flagstaff."

"So does that mean we are walking all the way to the Grand
Canyon?" Dallas asks.

"It's only 125 miles or so," I say. "Give or take."

She looks at me like I'm crazy, like I just suggested we flap our
arms and fly there.

"Six or seven days hard march," June says cheerfully.

Dallas braces herself on one of the central pipes and lifts her leg
and pulls up her jeans, showing that her ankle is still a little swollen.
"Not unless Woody is carrying me the whole way."

"Why, that *does* sound fun," I say with a small chuckle. "Having
you on my back for a week, telling me how to walk, telling me which
way to go, shouting at me to hurry up."

"Come on," she says. "Seriously. How the hell are we getting
there?"

I look at June. This is her plan and she stares right back at me, a
quirky smile on her face. It seems to say, I've got the big idea, but you
are the Arizona boy, so figure it out.

I don't mind her challenging me like that, I rather like it, but not
knowing where our relationship is at makes my mind work too hard
on it. We are partners in survival, that is clear, but is she looking for
something else before we can be closer? For me to prove myself.

I ignore the yammering in my mind and start talking aloud so I can think it through.

"No roads for us, at least not for a few days," I say. "We need to approach any crossroads with great care until Talia has turned her attention somewhere else."

June nods for me to continue.

"I say we parallel the highway but north a mile or two and we scrounge along the edges of Winslow," I continue. "It's going to be slow going with gimpy here, but that might not be a bad thing. We can't plan that far in advance, anyway. So we stay away from roads, stay away from Talia, scrounge and improvise as we go."

"So not much of a plan," Dallas says, a sour frown on her face.

I shrug. "Escape is the plan. Survival is the plan. What more do you need, Lonestar?" I haven't used her nickname much, the one I gave her when June was captured and we were trying to escape one of Talia's traps.

I know I wrote about how survival is not a plan so you might be wondering about the above statement. Let's just say there was some hindsight involved in that declaration, hindsight that I didn't have right now.

Dallas nods and smiles, letting out a sigh. "A steak would be nice, Diamondback," she says, using the nickname given to me by the Flagstaff psychotic, petty, wannabe warlord that Talia turned into a Z and June and I faced in the Apache Death Caves.

I got the nickname because of my ever-present Diamondbacks baseball cap which I lost in Winslow along with my jacket. I miss it, and my hand goes to my overlong hair trying vainly to push it out of my eyes. All this sun and I'm probably getting a sunburn on my face, and, if not that, it's going to be freckle city.

I don't think Dallas meant it, but it shifts my mood to thinking about the past, thinking about what has been lost, about things a lot more important than a hat.

I find June staring at me. She unties the bandana from her neck and says, "How about a haircut if there's time later?"

I blink and nod. A haircut is a pretty intimate gesture and I am hungry for intimacy with her.

"Lean down," she says, and takes her red bandana, folds it into a neat strip, and ties it around my head so it keeps my bangs out of my eyes.

When I stand up, I see Dallas staring at me with a tiny smile on her full lips and an eyebrow raised. She gives me a small nod before we all get back to work.

CHAPTER FOURTEEN

AFTER THE SIDES of the treehouse are down and stacked, we go to work on the floor. We need a hole in the center of the treehouse where we can drop the bomb from.

The sun is high in the sky and we aren't talking much, the labor and the growing heat of the day enough to use what energy we have. And we've been doing this for hours so we don't need to discuss it much.

The best wood was used for the floor, thicker and nailed to the joists, no open seams for us to pry under. We each go at the nails with our multi-tools, using the knife or flat-head screwdriver to dig around the nail and then the pliers to grip it.

My hands are still a mess from the zombie scratches and they itch, but not too much bleeding today so that's an improvement. Maybe this is kind of like physical therapy, so as these cuts heal they don't end up restricting my movements. Maybe, maybe not, but it helps me to think about it that way and feel better about how much it hurts.

It's good that I care more about how well my hands work than how they look, because they are gonna look all kinds of freaky with dozens of scars on each. I don't think my attitude would have been the same pre-apocalypse. The apocalypse has a habit of reframing your world in ways both big and small.

We target a board right in the middle of the treehouse. If we take all the nails out, then we can lift it, move it just far enough to create the gap we need, and then put it back down.

It's slow and monotonous. It's hard. But we have food. We are safe, just the stench of the Zs and the decomposing thousand-plus we already speared to deal with. And we are a "we." And that is the biggest thing of all.

The labor has relaxed me around the question of June. Don't get me wrong, my eyes linger on her lithe form whenever I see her. I want her. But it's just a background thing. My eyes will always linger on her and I will always want her regardless of the state of our relationship.

Once a nail is dug up enough for the pliers, you slip them in and pry it up, just a little. Get a better grip and pry some more. When the nail is up far enough you twist it to the side and keep prying. When the nail squeals as you pull it out of the wood, you know you are finally getting there and then it's on to another nail.

Having the wrong tools makes this ridiculously hard and that makes me wonder about Talia. Are we using the wrong tool with her? What is the right tool?

Back at the car dealership right outside of Winslow, I tried to shoot her, but she was prepared. I had never even thought of killing the living before, and this is what she drove me to. Is murder the right tool?

June wants to go to the Grand Canyon and make a stand there. Is that the right tool?

Are all these strategies for dealing with Talia like using pliers to try to pull up nails?

This whole Talia mess would be a hell of a lot easier if we knew what the right tool was, the right strategy. But people are a hell of a lot more complicated than nails.

It takes over an hour, but between the three of us, we get the board unnailed, make sure it will come up, and put it back in place.

We have a snack, I've graduated to the homemade jerky, and then we get to work on the bomb.

I give instructions and June and Dallas comply with unusual sobriety. It amuses me that this is what it takes—making a bomb.

First, we take three of our empty food cans, two with both the bottom and the top removed, and duct-tape those together making one tall can.

Next, we arrange the one-pound propane tanks around that tall can. We have six to use so we duct-tape three to the bottom of that tall can and three more on top.

Compared to what we have been doing, this is easy work, but we go extra slow. It's a bomb we are making, after all. But it's too tense and I don't like it. Before I think of it, I'm humming the tune to "If I Only Had a Brain" from *The Wizard of Oz* movie.

Before we really knew Dallas when we had escaped Talia at Phantom Ranch, Dallas had used it as a punch line when we were telling very bad zombie jokes.

They were like, so bad. That's what happens when you don't have the internet and have to make this kind of stuff up yourself.

"Seriously?" Dallas asks when she catches on to the bouncy tune, but there is a smile on her face.

I catch June's eye and she shakes her head but starts humming too, and what I hear makes me suspect she can sing because her pitch is far better than mine.

"Really?" Dallas asks June.

I hum louder as I pull the stick of dynamite from my pack. It's wrapped in rags and I keep humming as I unwrap it and inspect it. There are a few crystals of nitroglycerin clinging to the reddish cardboard at one end.

"Are you trying to tell me that we don't have any brains for attempting this?" Dallas asks.

I don't pay any attention to her, pulling out the blasting cap and fuse that is stored in another part of my backpack. The blasting cap is a thin metal cylinder and I insert the green safety fuse and crimp the end of the blasting cap tightly around the fuse, humming the whole time.

"I'm quite sure that is what you two are telling me," Dallas says, scooting back from June and I and the propane tanks.

I set the dynamite down, carefully, and use my knife to turn the rags into small pieces, the ripping sound strange accompaniment to our humming.

Our tall can is just over thirteen inches high and the stick of dynamite is eight inches long, so we take some of our nails and put them in the bottom, bend up some can tops, and add them. I then swaddle the bottom of the stick of dynamite in the rags I tore and put that in. June's humming has gotten louder and I'm quite sure she can sing and I really want to hear it.

It's not like we don't have music post-apocalypse. There's some on just about every phone lying around, just charge it up, scrounge some earphones and rock out. But it's been forever since I heard someone sing. I mean, I could do the singing, but it's really bad. I love music, but I am just not musical.

I hold the top of the dynamite while June and Dallas—after some coaxing—put in nails, can tops, pebbles, and anything else hard we can scrounge up here.

We go slow and it's a rather pleasant task. I'm not worried. The nitroglycerin crystals were few, making this fairly stable dynamite. It did fine in my backpack. Besides, if this bomb goes off, then that is the end of us. We won't be here and there won't be enough of us left to turn into Zs and it will be a quick death.

A little fatalistic, sure, but as endings go it wouldn't be a bad one.

A few minutes later Dallas is humming along with us and seems to have lightened up. As the song bounces along and reaches the end of a stanza, June sings, "If I only had a *bomb*."

Her voice is beautiful, the tone pure, and I can't help but smile.

I keep holding the dynamite and they keep filling in nails and other bits of stuff, and at the end of the next stanza, I join in with June in a low bass, "If I only had a *bomb.*"

My voice is not really bass, I'm pretty sure it's baritone, but I sing low like that because it feels safer. June flashes me a smile. Dallas sighs and shakes her head but keeps working.

A couple of stanzas later, Dallas starts making up lyrics, "Talia's such a bitch and I'd beat her with a stick, if I only had a bomb."

Dallas has a good voice too, lower than June's. So we start a round robin of bad lyrics with each one coming up with a couple of lines —usually about how we want to hurt Talia or disparaging her in creative ways—and then we all come in on "If I only had a bomb."

We end up laughing, the can full of nails, can tops, and miscellanea up to the level of the dynamite. It's good laughter, real laughter, and it goes on for a while.

Any laughter in an apocalypse.

Well, no mwahahas or cackling—that would likely make you a psychotic, petty, wannabe warlord—and schadenfreude is discouraged because it's just petty. Let me rephrase that:

Any *real* laughter in an apocalypse.

And we need it. And we laugh hard until our stomachs hurt. And then someone comes up with more lyrics and we sing some more and laugh some more.

For once in my life, I don't feel self-conscious about singing. I just let it come out, discarding the fake bass and singing comfortably.

And my singing is not great but it's not as bad as it normally would be with me worrying about it. And from a certain perspective, it's clear that I'm the third best singer of anyone for miles and miles.

"Well, we've got a bomb," Dallas says when we are finally laughed out. "Now what?"

"A few more finishing touches," I say. "We need a can top with a hole big enough for the fuse to fit through."

"Got it, boss," Dallas says and gets to work.

"Me?" June asks.

"Get some guyline and let's rig up a harness for this."

We take our time finishing the bomb, but every once in a while someone starts humming that tune and someone else laughs.

As apocalyptic afternoons go, it's a really good one. One we need because things always get complicated when you start blowing things up.

CHAPTER FIFTEEN

THE SUN IS EASING towards the horizon and the bomb is built and our backpacks repacked and an early dinner eaten. June has a pair of scissors out and is eying me critically.

Dallas catches my eye and gives me a small nod before saying, "I think I'll go spear me some Zs. For old-time's sake." She grabs one of the spears and clambers down the ladder humming "If I only had a bomb."

My stomach starts doing the cha-cha. Dallas left to give June and me space, which is nice, which is what a friend does, but there are so many ways to screw this conversation up. Especially with a relationship this new.

"Any requests?" June asks, a small smile on her beautiful face as she snips the scissors in the air.

It takes me a moment to realize that she's talking about the haircut. I shrug. "You have to look at me a lot more than I do, so make it something you don't hate looking at."

She smiles shyly. "That's quite impossible, Woody."

Her blue eyes are so deep and I get lost in them for a moment. I want to reach out and grab her, kiss her, undress her. I want to celebrate being alive with her.

"I love you, June Medina," I say, my heart pounding loud in my ears. I say it the same way I said it to her for the first time eighteen days ago when she gave herself up to Talia so Dallas and I could survive.

I say it so she can say back the same thing she said to me then, but she doesn't. "I know we need to talk more," she says instead, and it feels like my stomach is falling out.

"We do," I say, and now it's hard to keep looking into those eyes. Her lips are pursed and her forehead is furrowed.

"Mind if I cut while we do?" she asks.

"Sure," I say, and June nods, drapes the sleeping bag over my shoulders, and starts to work on the back of my head. "Maybe a beard trim if there is time. I'm looking a little too mountain-man for my taste."

I can't see her and she can't see me, and that is probably a good thing.

June combs my hair and I just want to groan from the pleasure of it. It's a simple intimacy, but a powerful one. It stops too soon and she starts trimming, the scissors cool against my neck. I can feel the scissors cutting and hear the snip-snip. It's a welcome change from the grumble of the Zs which is louder now that Dallas is down there. A whoop rises up every now and then as she gets another one.

I don't want to say anything, but I know we don't have a ton of time so after a few breaths, I ask, "Are we okay?"

June stops and I can hear her take a deep breath and sighs. "No, Woody," she says. "This is a terrible mess we've gotten ourselves into, but no one is okay anymore. I'm not okay, you're not okay, so how can 'we' be okay?"

"You know what I mean," I say. "You told me a little of what you went through when I was surrounded in Winslow, when I was sick. But..."

I don't know how to continue. She starts combing my hair again and I feel a little self-conscious. It's been too long since I had a chance to wash it in any way. The last time back at the Earthship in the 40s. I know it's greasy and unappealing, hard to imagine it's helping me plead my case for continuing our relationship.

"You don't understand?" she asks, her tone gentle.

"I understand how hard it is losing someone you love," I say, my words slow as I do my best to choose them carefully. "I know what it feels like to give all you've got to get them back and being terrified it's not enough."

"Right," she says, the scissors snipping. "I'm glad you get it."

She's not being clear. I have to assume this is because of the difficulty of the topic, something about her past that makes it hard to express herself. And Talia being the relationship she was in before me must be part of it.

"But, June," I say, turning slightly because I want to see her, but then realizing it's probably better this way for her and turning back. "That just made me want to be with you more. That made me know how precious whatever time we have together is."

I don't say that she's obviously gone somewhere else with it. Dallas told me she needs space, and I am afraid to push her too far.

"But Woody," she says, her voice tight and strained. "We are in this situation, right now, because we stopped. Because we got lost in being with each other. Because we had our night at the Grand Canyon after you rescued me. Because we had those rest days in that house on the cinder cone. Because..."

She's not cutting my hair or combing it anymore, and she's breathing hard. She's blaming herself for the delays, for giving in to a few moments of pleasure. This may not be all of it, but it is at least part of it.

"This is not an excuse," I say, "but we didn't know what was coming. We didn't know Talia would be following us out of the Grand Canyon so soon or taking over the Flagstaff gang so easily. Dallas and I had walked so many miles that our feet were a wreck. We needed the time. We needed the rest. But I see what you are saying, that we should have moved on faster. Especially at the 40s."

"I'm glad you understand," she says, gently turning my head and resuming the haircut on the left side.

"June, I don't regret a moment I've spent with you," I say. "And while the past is clear, what we could have done better is clear, what is not clear is what we would have run into if we hadn't stopped. We have no idea what other dangers we would have faced less rested and less prepared."

"Woody, this is not some silly rom-com," she says. "This is a hard life in an insane world. We can't just fall into each other's arms every chance we get."

"I think that's exactly what we should be doing," I say. "When we are safe. When we can find moments where it makes sense. I'm not saying we shouldn't have moved on faster from the 40s. We should have. I regret not being stronger. But I think we've both learned that lesson."

"So you want to pretend that none of that happened," she says, still again. "That Winslow didn't happen. That Talia's game didn't happen... isn't happening."

I can't stand not seeing her so I turn around and take her face in my hands. "No, I don't. I know what kind of world we live in and that makes finding you that much more of a miracle. That makes every day of survival that we have together worthy of celebration. I love you. I want to express that and show that in every way possible. I want to fight with you until we have no strength left. I want to share a sleeping bag and just hold you. I want to hold your hand just to know you are here and with me. And, yes, I want the physical stuff and the silly rom-com romance when we are safe.

"I had been alone for a long time when we met. Every day with you has been better than the days without you. I want all of you that I can get, but if friendship is all you have to give, I will find a way to live with that and be glad of it."

After the words are out, I feel such embarrassment, heat rushing to my cheeks. I gave a speech. A silly, romantic speech. I am not giving her space. I am not giving her time.

But how much time do we have?

It's clear we are going to survive today, but what about tomorrow?

She's blinking, her lips moving like she's trying to find words, her nostrils flaring as she breathes deeply. The seconds tick by slowly, neither of us saying anything.

"This is all my fault," she finally says with a sniff, her ocean blue eyes darting away from mine. "All. My. Fault."

"No," I say, drawing her into a hug. "It was my idea to stop at that Earthship. I'm sorry. I thought we had time. We might have gotten away if we had gone south after Meteor Crater, but we all decided to turn around. It's not just—"

"No!" she says, pushing me away and wiping at her eyes. "Talia! *She* is all my fault."

I'm staring at her trying to understand what she is saying. "What do you mean?" I ask quietly.

"There were signs, you know," she begins, and then bites her lower lip. "In Afghanistan. In the Army. She... she had a reputation of being a little volatile, a little too happy to be there, and I—"

She wraps her arms around her chest, and when her eyes meet mine, I feel a shiver of fear run through me. "But I had seen too much," she continues. "I needed something. I needed somebody and she pursued me. Hard. It was flattering. It was distracting. I..."

She trails off and gets up, walking to the now railing-less edge of the treehouse looking to the south over the rough land and the splash of darker green from the Little Colorado. As the sun gets closer to the horizon, the colors darken and richen.

I have questions. So many questions, but I just get up and stand next to her, feeling how high we are, how dangerous this treehouse is without the short walls. Feeling how dangerous this moment is for June. For us.

"I knew it wasn't a forever thing," she says quietly. "Those kinds of relationships rarely are. They are a way through the madness. A way to survive."

My stomach feels like it just dived into the roiling sea of Zs below. Is she telling me that is what our relationship is? Just a way through the madness. A way to survive.

"And after the Zs," she says, taking a deep breath and letting out a long sigh. "After we saw what was going on and survived the insanity of the first few days, she... she changed." June glances up at me and her eyes are haunted. "Well... I liked to tell myself that she changed. And I guess she did, but it was more like the layers of civility were washed away by the apocalypse and it showed who she really was."

"I think that's true for all of us," I say gently. "It shows who we really are without the guardrails and consequences of civilization."

She gives me a small, bitter smile and nods, looking back out over the desert. "Except, I had seen her in war," she says. "The least civil thing we humans do, and I knew who she was and still I was surprised."

We're not talking about our relationship anymore but hers and Talia's. It would be a bit hyperbolic to say I'd rather be back in Winslow facing that zombie horde for the first time, but only a bit. This is a profoundly uncomfortable conversation for both of us. But that's part of a relationship, part of demonstrating love. To be there for those profoundly uncomfortable conversations.

And I do love her. I realize that this feeling was forged in the madness of the last thirty-three days, that it might have taken that pressure to create our relationship, but how it happened has no bearing on what I feel and what I want.

"And then we met," she says, nodding and biting her lip again as she stares into the distance, another Dallas whoop rising up from the snarls and stench below us.

"I hope that's a good thing," I say.

She takes a deep breath. "It is, Woody. You're a good man and I'm lucky to have met you."

She goes silent and my heart is clanging in my head.

"But..." I prompt.

She turns and stares into my eyes, her gaze hard. "But this is my fault. Talia is *my* fault. This whole goddamn mess is *my* fault." Now her voice is loud and her words are shooting out of her. "I'm the one that made you prove your fungus theory about the Zs so we ended up at the Grand Canyon. And we ended up being chased down in the Canyon. And we ended up running into Talia. And now we've been fighting her and escaping her this whole time.

"This is all my fault. Can't you see that?"

I smile at her and I hope it looks gentle and compassionate. I had these thoughts myself but my spin on it is very different. While this is literally all June's fault, I would be dead without her and God knows what would have happened to June. But I don't say any of that because she needs to get this out and this is exactly the space that Dallas told me she needed.

"You almost died in Winslow," she continues. "If this game continues, you *will* die. And if Talia has her way it will be me doing it to prevent you from turning into a Z. That's what she wants. That's what's coming for you and Dallas."

She pauses for a breath and I open my mouth to speak but her words don't stop. "I know you think she wants me back, Woody, but that is not it. I committed the cardinal sin in her eyes. I rejected her. Repeatedly. She wants me dead. But she wants me broken first. She wants me to end Dallas, to end you, before she ends me herself."

Tears are forming in her eyes and her nostrils are flaring, she's breathing so hard. "That is Talia. That is what she wants. This is all my fault."

Space be damned, I grab her and hold her as tightly as I dare. She pushes me away, but only briefly and then tears come and she holds me tightly as she cries.

CHAPTER SIXTEEN

LOVING SOMEONE, needing someone, means that you will have to let them go someday. Unless you are "lucky" and both die in a—oh, I don't know—an explosion, you have to say goodbye, you have to let go.

This is an essential truth about our reality, pre- or post-apocalypse. We all know it, but we all like to ignore the fact, pretending that forever is possible.

Earlier in my journals, I think I mentioned that I was in a previous post-apocalypse relationship. That it ended badly. And "ended badly" is a whole lot of glossing over a whole lot of terrible stuff.

Her name was Anna and she was shy and sweet and being with her did what June said about her relationship with Talia did while they were in the Army. It helped me through the madness. It helped me survive.

Well, it helped her too. I'm sure of it. At least for a while.

I'm not sure that I loved her, and I think I would have gotten there in time, but I cared very much for her and I watched her die. Her and my mentor, the man known as Q who taught me what I know about electronics and explosives and jury-rigging your way through the apocalypse. I watched them both die.

I'm not ready to write that story yet. Partially because it was traumatic, but mostly because I had some responsibility for their fate. I regret what I didn't do and that terrible moment has shaped how I've been since then.

It drove me away from Phoenix. I left that tribe and its psychotic, petty, wannabe warlord—and let me tell you, that wasn't easy. The petty and psychotic don't like to let go. Talia is not the only one, not by a long shot.

I was on my own for all that time until I got to Flagstaff and that dog food plant and June. And I fell for June hard as we met, as she saved my life, as we shared dog food, and as I saved her from the Flagstaff psychotic, petty, wannabe warlord.

As June cries, as I hold her, memories of Anna and Q flit through my mind and the shame of my failure heats my cheeks.

I have no doubt that I love June, but now I have to wonder if the strength of my emotions isn't, at least in part, me making up for what happened with Anna.

I know earlier I said I didn't care what the conditions were that created these feelings, but what if Anna and her fate were one of those conditions? What if how I failed her and Q is what has driven me to go to such extremes for June and Dallas?

The thought shakes me as her body shakes against mine.

My view of June as fearless, as the toughest person I know, is tempering as she cries. She is strong, but she is human. She has moments of vulnerability. Of course she does.

But standing there in the cell tower treehouse, I don't extend that courtesy to myself. Q and Anna fell to Zs and I didn't do enough to prevent it. Back in Winslow, I took insane risks to save Dallas—was that just a reaction to Q and Anna dying?

Is my bond with June just a reaction?

"What's wrong?" June asks between sniffs.

I realize that I'm not holding her very tightly anymore. "I've made some terrible mistakes, too," I say.

She pulls back a little and looks up at me, her eyes searching my face, but I can't meet her gaze. She draws me away from the edge and we sit down, our legs crossed, facing each other.

"Tell me," she says.

"You won't like me anymore," I say, because I don't like myself when I remember this.

"Do you still like me after what I just said?" she asks.

"Of course," I say.

"Tell me." she repeats.

Early on in our relationship—and bizarrely that is just thirty-three days ago—the past was off the table for conversation, just too much, just too painful.

But now the past is relevant to our present, to our relationship.

I had a moment with Dallas on the South Rim of the Grand Canyon after we had survived our insane and foolish rafting trip down the Colorado where I wanted to confess all of this to Dallas, where I needed someone to really know me. She told me we all had done things and that if I regretted it that set me apart from the psychotic, petty, wannabe warlords. She told me, "Save that for your girlfriend once we rescue her."

So there on the plywood floor of our cell tower treehouse, I confess to June. I tell her how my inaction and cowardice led to Anna's and Q's deaths. I tell her that was why I was alone when we met. That that was what I was running from.

It spills out of me. Not every detail, but all the ones that count. Enough for her to get the shape of my shame. Enough for her to see how weak I can be.

After it is over, she wipes the tears off my cheeks. I didn't even realize I had been crying. She gives me a wan smile and nods.

There is silence between us, but I'm not scared that she'll run away from me. Well... ignore the fact that we are under siege from thousands of Zs at the moment and she literally can't run away from me. The fear has left me. At least for the moment. What is left is something softer, something more expansive.

Yes, I love June on many levels. Yes, I want her. But the feeling I have now is one of acceptance. She is right here, right now. She's holding my hands, a myriad of emotions playing on her lovely face. She has witnessed my deepest shame and not freaked out.

"Better?" she asks.

I purse my lips and nod. "Yeah. I wish I had done more. I wish they hadn't died, but that's in the past. I can't change it."

June licks her lips and nods. "And I can't change my mistakes with Talia. We have to let that shit go."

And while "shit" is the official word of the apocalypse, maybe "we have to let that shit go" should be the official saying.

A reflex in me wants to ask her about "us," about where we are, if there is a Woody and June anymore. But it's just a brief flittering fear. There is clearly a Woody and June because we are having this experience, and trying to endlessly define our relationship and label it isn't going to help anything.

I love June, and my job, along with survival and laughter, of course, is to find ways to express that love that are appropriate to the situation.

I love Dallas too, but in different ways, and my job with her is the same.

Survive. Laugh. Spend time with them both.

Our eyes lock and it feels like volumes are being spoken. I can feel her love, like it's a tangible force, but I can also feel the pain of her trauma, of her past.

Of course, my experience with Anna and Q has informed how I am acting and feeling now. How could it not? This is the way being human works. And of course June's experiences with Talia are changing how she is with me.

Life happens. You change.

I still regret what happened in Phoenix. I still feel the shame, but maybe, just maybe, it won't be defining me anymore.

"You all done with super heartfelt sharing time?" Dallas calls from the ladder. "Because I'm tired of standing on this ladder waiting for you two to just kiss and get it over with."

June chuckles and leans in and kisses me. It's not a romantic kiss or a passionate one, but it's an extraordinarily intimate one. As if that kiss is sealing the bond between us that came from what we both shared. As if that kiss can say more than words ever could.

"Okay," June calls after our lips part. "He's been kissed, come on up."

"Good," Dallas says as she climbs up and steps on the platform. She stands there leaning on the spear, the end blunted and dark with zombie goo. "I just want to say, I've done many terrible things too. Like when I followed you two innocent cuties up to the North Rim doing the evil Talia's dark bidding."

She pauses and takes a deep breath and lets out a noisy sigh. "And I feel *terrible* about it." She says it dramatically, dripping with faux emotion.

"How long have you been listening?" I ask.

She takes a step forward and says, "Long enough to find out you aren't perfect, Woody. And let me tell you, it's a goddamn relief."

"What?!" I ask.

"A relief, I say," Dallas says, flopping down next to us. "No one's perfect. No one's a saint. And if they look to be even halfway there, something is really wrong."

I just stare at her blinking. I have nothing to say. Not that I don't believe her about the no one's perfect thing, I do. I just can't imagine how I have appeared to be anything even close to perfect or saintly.

Dallas crawls over and grabs her pack. "Okay, so I've been saving this." She pulls out a small stainless-steel flask. "But I think this is an occasion." She unscrews the lid, takes a sniff, and a smile lights up her face, turning those frown lines into smile lines.

"To Woody here not being perfect," she says, raising the flask and flashing me a wicked smile. "And to being over his 'I don't know if

June wants me' funk. And to bombing the shit out of some Zs in the morning."

She takes a sip and passes the flask. It's whiskey and I'm not much of a hard alcohol drinker, but I gladly take it hoping they aren't noticing how much I'm blushing. I take a sip and enjoy the burn as it slides down.

After she has the flask back, Dallas says, "So, I missed most of your confession, Woody. Care to share it again? I'm your best friend, after all."

I shake my head. "I tried to tell you. After we climbed out of the canyon, after our rafting trip. You wouldn't hear it."

Her forehead furrows and her eyes narrow. "Fair enough. What else can we talk about?" She takes another sip but doesn't pass the flask this time. "I know. How about we all share how we lost our virginity. You go first, Woody."

They are both staring at me and my cheeks flush red and this time I'm sure they notice it. Their laughter rings out as the sun slides below the horizon.

CHAPTER SEVENTEEN

WE TALK INTO THE NIGHT, Dallas sharing the flask some more, the whiskey loosening our tongues. I don't tell them how I lost my virginity, but we do share stories, both pre- and post-apocalypse. The kind of stories that real friends tell and real friends listen to. The kind of things that we all need to have witnesses for.

We don't talk about Talia or my time in Phoenix or anything too awful. It's just three friends having a chat and it's nice.

June joins me in the sleeping bag and I don't overthink it for once. We just sleep and we are up before dawn. It's time to blow up some Zs and get the hell out of here.

The air is cool and the stars are starting to fade as the horizon lightens to the east. There is a breeze that is helping reduce the zombie stench levels but making me cold outside of the sleeping bag.

We all check our backpacks, make sure everything is where it should be. Make sure our weapons are loaded and ready. Put our backpacks on. Move the treehouse floorboard and open a hole onto the sluggish mass below us.

They are waking up too.

I mean, the Zs don't really sleep, not in a recognizable way, but their activity levels slow way down like they are conserving energy.

I carefully go over the guyline we have tied around the bomb, making sure it is tight, and I tie the other end of it to my belt, attaching the bomb to me. We have one stick of dynamite in the tall tin can we made surrounded by nails, can tops, and other bits of debris. Duct-taped around the can are six one-pound tanks of propane. I go over it in my head again. The Zs are packed tight, and this should create a fireball. How big? I'm not too sure, but I am hopeful that between the fireball and the shrapnel there won't be much left of the Winslow zombie horde.

I sit on the near end of our stacked wood and metal street signs, and June, with gloves on, carefully lowers the bomb into the hole in the floor. The guyline goes taut but she keeps a hold of it. I feel the pull on my belt.

We discussed the plan in detail while we made the bomb, so we are not saying anything. Hope is busy buzzing around, and this time I can't help but let it in. This has to help. We lost a whole day of zombie spearing and this has to do better than the six hundred or so Zs we would have gotten that way.

"Ready?" Dallas asks. She has a lighter in her hand and is leaning over the hole, the bomb dangling just below the surface.

June lets go of the guyline and joins me over on the reinforced area. I pull my knife from my belt and slide it under the guyline. We have about ten seconds of fuse, which should be plenty.

"Ready," I say. It's a tense moment and I kind of want to lighten it with a joke, but it's probably not appropriate, and, besides, I can't think of one.

Dallas flicks her lighter to life, leans down and touches the flame to the fuse and I hear the distinct angry hissing of a fuse burning.

While she lunges for safety, I pull my knife across the guyline and the bomb falls.

"Nine," June says, starting the countdown.

A rewarding splat-crunch floats up from below and the Zs start making more noise. Are they curious? Do they wonder what it is?

"Eight," June intones. "Seven."

I check and we are all well within the boundaries of the stacked boards and signs. I look over to the hole and wish sliding that board back in place had been part of the plan.

"Six. Five."

But maybe I'm overthinking the power of this explosion. Maybe it won't be much of anything and we'll have days of spearing left to do.

"Four. Three."

I catch June's eye and there is a grin on her face, a sure sign of hope. And that worries me. Hope flips to despair, too damn quick.

"Two. One."

As planned, we are all facing each other. We lean in and down so our backpacks are the most exposed part of us.

"Zero!" June shouts.

But nothing happens.

"What the hell..." Dallas says, sitting up.

"Get down!" I say. "Maybe the fuse is burning slow."

So we stay there like turtles with our protective shells as the seconds tick by. Ten. Twenty. Thirty.

"Shit," June says. "Could it take this long?"

"I don't see how," I say. "But we need to give it more time. Just in case."

Dallas curses and I can feel all of our hope twisting on us, flipping to despair. This didn't work out like we had expected. Now all we've done is wasted a day assembling the inert thing that's down among the Zs now.

"What happened?" Dallas asks.

I shrug. "The fuse has to have failed or it was a bad blasting cap. Can't be anything else."

"Now what?" June asks.

We're sitting up and they are both staring at me. My brain searches for options. We need fire to get to the dynamite. But how?

"Any whiskey left?" I ask Dallas.

She shakes her head. "We finished it last night."

There's something about Dallas's expression, how her eyes dart away, but I don't give it a second thought, but June does.

"Any *other* alcohol in that pack of yours?" June asks.

Dallas sighs. "Some vodka. Saving it for medicinal purposes."

June looks at me. "Will that help?"

"It might," I say. "Let me see."

Dallas grumbles and takes off her pack, digs out a flask, and hands it to me. This one is about ten ounces and almost full, twice as big as the whiskey flask. Like when Talia and company were chasing us, we could make a small Molotov cocktail out of this and drop some fire on top of the bomb, but will it work?

"We need something glass," I say.

June goes over to the built-in cabinets and comes up with an old soda bottle.

A plan pops into my head. It's stupid and dangerous, but it will work. It will trigger the bomb. It might also get us a face full of shrapnel.

I tell them my plan. We can risk our lives setting the bomb off or we can go back to spearing all day for at least another five days.

"I'm in," June says. "Let's blow them up."

"Me too," Dallas says with a grin. "I guess you could consider this use of my vodka *medicinal.*"

CHAPTER EIGHTEEN

THE TREEHOUSE FLOOR and our reinforced layers have been rearranged a bit for our second attempt with the bomb.

The boards are now stacked up right next to the hole, which is not very wide anymore. This is important. The sun is fully up and we took a break and ate some food. We needed to wait for the light for this part.

Dallas spotted the bomb among the roiling mass of fungus-heads. Just a glimpse, but it's right where we expected it to be lying on its side.

June's got her rifle out and the soda bottle Molotov cocktail awaits lighting.

This is a whole lot more complicated now, and a lot more risky.

"So we got the plan?" I ask.

June nods. "You do the count," she says to me. "On one, Dallas lights the Molotov, and on three, I shoot the bomb, one of the propane tanks, specifically, and Dallas drops the Molotov. On four, you yank us both back so we don't get our faces burned off. And then the burning alcohol from the Molotov mixes with the gas from the punctured propane tank and boom city!"

She ends in a sweet smile that makes this so much more complicated for me.

I had lobbied for the role with the Molotov, but Dallas wouldn't hear of it, saying the strongest of us had to be in the anchor role.

"So let's do a dry run," I say.

We are all standing. Dallas on the reinforced floor right next to the hole. June is straddling it so she can shoot from a standing position. And I am behind them both holding ropes that are tied around their shoulders like a harness. The waist won't do, too low a center of gravity.

I pull the ropes taut and squat down, lowering my own center of gravity.

"One," I say, and Dallas pantomimes lighting her can of peas which is a stand in for the Molotov cocktail.

"Two," I say, and Dallas nods, letting me know the cocktail lit okay.

"Three." And June makes a "pew" noise like a kid would do with a toy gun.

And that actually hits me pretty hard. Not long after we met, after we survived the first zombie attack on the South Rim, I explained to June the childhood accident when my brother and I were young and playing cowboys and Indians. I was like, six, and had my father's gun. I made a "pew" noise like that and accidentally shot my brother in the arm.

It's how I ended up in the apocalypse hating guns.

But I shake it off. "Four." I pull back hard on the ropes and both of them tumble onto the reinforced area and me.

I look around and June's foot is still over the opening.

"Let's do it again," I say. "We need all body parts in the safety zone."

"You're so sweet to care about our body parts," Dallas says with a leering grin, her face close to mine. There's been no more talk about throuples or any other form of polyamory, just the usual Dallas griping about turning into a spinster.

It makes me wonder what June and Dallas talked about when I was down spearing Zs. I feel a stirring of jealousy but shove it down hard. June and I have arrived at a clear-as-mud undefined relationship, and jealousy would clear that up real quick—as in no more possibility of intimacy.

"I would prefer we leave here with all our body parts," I say to Dallas, smiling back as if I don't get her drift.

We practice the maneuver again, and Dallas has a leg over the hole, and again, and they both have feet over the hole.

I'm feeling pretty good, but I am not quite up to full strength yet. This is not working.

"Let's move the ropes to your waists," I say.

"Not worried about our center of gravity?" June asks. I had explained the reasoning for roping them around their shoulders earlier.

"He is so sweet to worry about our centers of gravity," Dallas says. She has clearly got something going on. And I give her some latitude because it's never fun being the third wheel, although I don't know if that characterization is even accurate anymore. Plus we've been stuck in the treehouse for five days. The isolation has to be taking its toll.

"It's my strength I'm worried about," I say. "But the shoulder thing isn't working, so let's try it."

She nods and I work with both of them, getting the ropes around their waists. Dallas doesn't make any rude comments as I tie the rope to the back of her belt.

We go through the routine again. I have to pull a lot harder, and we all end up in a jumble with June's head banging into my crotch and I understand what had triggered Dallas. Random body parts touching between healthy adults.

She's horny.

And she's been stuck up here with us for days.

And I'm just about well enough to be horny too.

But there is a time for such things, and this is not it.

June and Dallas are in the clear this time, but my head is over an unreinforced area. So, we rearrange our stack of boards and metal signs so it extends farther but isn't quite as thick. We had more than we needed so it should be fine.

We try it again and this time Dallas's ample curves are pressed against me.

"How's everyone's body parts?" she calls.

"I'm good," June says.

"Me too," I say.

Dallas pushes on my chest as she levers herself up. "I'm good," she says with a wicked grin, her eyes connecting with mine. "All body parts present and ready for action."

Dallas is an attractive woman, and early on after she followed June and me out of the Grand Canyon, she made me an offer of uncomplicated and frequent physical intimacy. Sure, she was working for Talia at the time and, sure, later on she told me, "I'm nobody's second choice," but this is the mercurial Dallas we are talking about.

Not that it mattered then. She offered sex, but I wanted June. I wanted more. Now that we are all as close as we are, I don't have a clue what she is hinting at.

I catch June smiling at me after Dallas gets up. I'm not sure what kind of smile it is. It's not a full-on happy smile, but it's not an ironic one either.

What is clear to me right then is that I don't understand women, and I most certainly don't understand these two.

"Are we good to go?" June asks.

I nod. "Yeah. Let's double-check everything and do it."

CHAPTER NINETEEN

I TAKE another look at our surroundings. I've seen this view many times, and as Arizona goes, its beauty is mild, but a safe haven in the apocalypse, even one where you are under siege by a few thousand zombies, is a rarity.

Maybe it's because we took the three-feet walls down and I can really see the view now, even when sitting down with only the cell tower supports in the way. Maybe it's because we're about to do something really dangerous. Maybe it's because we are hopefully leaving soon. Whatever it is, I really see it.

To the east are the inert twin smokestacks of the coal power plant right past Joseph City. I-40 runs through the desert south of us with railroad tracks just to the other side and the winding cut of the Little Colorado River beyond that, scraggly bushes that have some real green crowding the edge and competing for the scant desert water.

To the west is a small tabletop mesa carved out of reddish sandstone, providing uncharacteristic flair to the otherwise flat and gently sloping land.

The Navajo reservation is to the north, the White Mountains to the south, Holbrook to the east, and Winslow to the west.

Arizona has a lot of "in the middle of nowhere" places and this is one.

Ostensibly, I am resting for the big event, but I'm staring at the landscape trying to distract myself from Dallas's not-so-subtle advances. I have to wonder if I'm being handed off, being traded to another team without consultation.

Woody and Dallas versus the Apocalypse just doesn't have the same ring to it as Woody and June. I thought I had found my romantic "happily ever after considering it's the apocalypse."

There's a part of me, that stupid male "spread your seed" hornball monster, that would be perfectly happy with Dallas.

No. That's not fair. Dallas is capable and beautiful and I really don't mind her sharp edges and sarcasm. You usually don't have to wonder what's on her mind.

Let me try again. I would be lucky to have Dallas as a romantic partner, my returning primal urges quite happy about it, but my heart, it wants June. Just June. Always June.

Perhaps monogamy is horribly outdated in this era. If humans survive the Zs, I expect it will have to be for a time for the health of the gene pool, but my heart doesn't care about any of that.

It's all June for my romantic side.

I shake it off and start cataloging the landscape again. The Jack Rabbit Trading Post is just to the west and that's probably worth scrounging after we get out of here and before we wander off into the desert for June's grand plan. There's also a few homes dotting the land near here that could provide support, but it would be best to go through them quickly and leave the area.

"Um..." June begins from behind me. "Woody. I... I think you need to see this."

I get up and walk over. June is by the hole in the treehouse staring down. I join her and what I see is impossible. The Zs are still a swirling mass of rotting flesh and unending hunger below us, but there is an opening, a gap. Right around the bomb.

I can see it clearly sitting on the ground. Well, not the ground, really, but the trampled remains of some of the speared Zs. So the "ground" the bomb is resting on is rotting flesh and old dirty bits of clothing. They've made a gap around the bomb, which is lying on its side, several of the green one-pound propane tanks clearly visible. And that gap is slowly getting bigger like a school of shambling fish moving away from something it just figured out is dangerous.

My sci-fi indoctrinated brain makes some quick and terrifying leaps and I shout, "Now! We need to do this now!"

OKAY, so the Zs have their fresh-brains radar and can track humans without seeing them, hearing them, or smelling them. A single Z's radar isn't that accurate, maybe a hundred yards. But, as their numbers gather, that range gets longer and longer.

Like they form a group mind of some sort and their individual fresh-brains radars become like the array of radio telescopes in New Mexico.

I've explained this before, but bear with me. The salient fact is that their minds are working together to form a group mind.

This is clear. I've seen it over and over. While I don't understand the mechanics behind it, the results are undeniable.

So, from there, is it a far leap to think that while one Z is a dumb shambling embodiment of hunger, that a group of Zs might be a little smarter, that a horde of thousands of them might actually become intelligent?

If their fungus brains can cooperate on the fresh-brains radar, doesn't it stand to reason that it can cooperate in other ways?

After months contained in smaller groups in Winslow by Talia and company, then all together for the last five days as they tried to eat us, could their group brain have grown intelligent enough to figure out the thing we dropped on them is meant to destroy them?

Maybe one of them can smell the dynamite, and another one of them understands the destructive power of propane, and yet another knows what the fuse is and what it means.

Or maybe they recognized the pattern that every time something came down from the treehouse it was to their detriment.

"The fuse fell out," Dallas says, her small binoculars to her face. "That's what happened."

But could one of them have pulled the burning fuse out? Could the Zs' fungus brains retain something of their living mind, enough that these thousands figured out what we are trying to do to them?

It's an academic question. They are moving away from the bomb as if the mind of the horde is slowly changing, prioritizing survival over eating us.

"Positions!" I yell, grabbing the Molotov cocktail and handing it to Dallas, checking the ropes still tied around their waists, pushing back the terror that's starting to well up in me.

How much harder will it be to survive against intelligent groups of Zs? How long until they learn—or relearn—how to climb ladders and nowhere is safe?

"Ready," June says, straddling the gap, the rifle to her shoulder.

"Ready," Dallas calls, the Molotov in one hand, a lit lighter in the other.

I test the ropes one more time and shout, "One!"

Dallas lights the Molotov, the rag sticking out of the end of the soda bottle flaring to life as the flames eagerly consume the alcohol.

"Two!"

June fires and I hear the distinct "ping" sound of the bullet hitting metal.

"Three!"

Dallas drops the Molotov cocktail.

"Four!" I yank hard and they tumble on me and we all go down.

And then all hell breaks loose.

THE EARTH DOESN'T MOVE beneath us and we are not awash in flames, but I think we're close to achieving a Hollywood explosion.

I hear it first, a deafening boom, and then I feel a wash of heat and hear and feel shrapnel hitting the platform below us and pinging off the metal structure of the cell tower.

The whole tower shakes briefly like it's an earthquake and I have a brief moment of terror wondering whether Dallas's fear of the tower falling over will come to something.

The fetid stench changes to something that is still quite fetid but with a huge dose of charred added to the disgusting bouquet.

My ears are ringing but I hear, or rather don't hear, the distinct lack of snarling.

"Everyone okay?" I ask, my voice coming out as a rough shout.

"I've got all my body parts," Dallas says, her head lying on my chest. "Would you like to do an inspection, Woody?"

I ignore her. "June?" I ask, her backpack is pressed to my side.

She doesn't reply right away and I surge up, pushing Dallas off me. "June!"

I reach for her, but she pushes my hands away. "I'm fine," she says, her eyes distant. "Just thinking. How... how the hell did they do that? How did they know?"

"I've got a theory," I say, willing my pounding heart to slow. The thought of her lying there dead, a piece of shrapnel sticking out of her temple, was more than I could bear. It was like an elephant sitting on my chest.

I don't elaborate, I go to the hole and look down.

I see zombies, or rather lots of parts of zombies, but no movement.

I want to cry with relief. It worked. The bomb worked.

"What the hell..." Dallas says from behind me.

I twist around and she is standing at the edge of the platform staring down at the ground, June next to her.

I walk over and my still fast beating heart almost stops.

There are zombies, whole and well, but they are leaving. It's a group of maybe a hundred Zs in a tight-packed bunch heading towards the west, back towards Winslow.

June points, and another pod of them, a similar size, is wandering to the east, towards Joseph City and Holbrook.

And another pod is wandering towards the north into the desert.

"Pod" seems to be the right word. The one you would use when describing a group of whales or dolphins. "School" might work or "flock," but it's pod that my brain holds on to.

We spot two more pods, all heading off in different directions meaning at least five hundred Zs survived and these seem to be smarter Zs. They somehow learned that we weren't worth the trouble and gave up.

The Zs gave up.

Dallas lets out a string of curses.

June grabs my arm and squeezes like she's afraid she'll fall.

"What have we done?" I mumble.

CHAPTER TWENTY

"I THINK THEY HATE US," Dallas says as the zombie pod heading west shambles its way out of sight. It got on the I-40 and stayed on it as if it knew that was the quickest way back to Winslow, that there would be brains to eat back there.

"I think they're scared of us," June whispers.

We haven't moved from our perch on the treehouse fifty feet up the cell phone tower. We are witnessing zombies with intelligence, and that seems to have robbed us of our intelligence.

The sun is up and a cool breeze is stirring the air, but I barely feel the cold, and the bright sunshine seems wan and ineffective.

"I think we're screwed," I say.

The one factor that has made this zombie apocalypse survivable is the sheer single-minded stupidity of the Zs. If they are growing a brain—or a group brain, rather—then we really are screwed.

We stand there watching the pods leave. Their paths wander a bit, like a toddler trying to learn how to use its legs properly, but they always get back on track and keep going in a consistent direction. As if each pod has a chosen destination. None of them turn back towards us and we are free to go but are just too stunned.

"What is your theory?" June finally asks, her worried ocean-blue eyes finding mine as she chews on her lower lip.

I explain it. These Zs, after so long a confinement together, honed a superior group mind, and then the large numbers of them all after us for these days and that group mind became intelligent.

"So... they knew it was a bomb?" Dallas asks.

I shrug. "Maybe. Or they realized that every time something came down from the treehouse they were hurt."

"So it's all Talia's fault," Dallas says, her lip curling up a bit at Talia's name. "She confined them together for so long that their stupid group mind got less stupid."

I don't point out that Dallas was there in Winslow with Talia and company when these Zs were confined, that she participated in it.

I shrug again. My theory is untestable.

"What... what if this is just their natural progression?" June asks.

"What?" I ask.

"You know," she says. "This many months in with zombies this mature, maybe this is just what happens."

I remember the water tank up at the North Rim that had the fungus growing in it and drinking it had killed and turned into Zs a group of otherwise healthy survivors. The fungus found another way to get us.

Maybe these zombie pods are a natural evolution of the fungus-head brains of theirs.

"That would mean this is happening everywhere," I say, my voice just above a whisper.

"Shit," Dallas intones. "We are screwed. We are all totally and epically screwed."

WE DON T STAY up in the treehouse for much longer. We've been at this too long to let even this crazy of a turn keep us still. After all the pods are out of sight, we make sure we have everything and down the ladder we go.

Dallas keeps one of the spears and is using it as a walking stick. Her ankle is a lot better, but it's not all the way healed, and we have a lot of miles to go.

The ground at the center of the cell tower where the bomb blew is blackened and charred, some of the metal equipment bent and twisted from the blast. Beyond the center of the blast area are body parts, everywhere. Arms, legs, hands, feet, torsos, heads, and lots and lots of bits of unidentifiable rotting chunks of fungus-infected flesh. What remains standing of all that gear is plastered with so much of the zombie remains that you can't really tell it's metal anymore.

It is disgusting.

But on the bright side, it did clear out some of the mess of zombie flesh left over from all of that spearing. "Some of it" being the key phrase there. I won't go into details, but just imagine what was left under the cell tower after all the twelve hundred or so speared zombies got trampled for a good long while and then a bomb went off. Not pretty and not something I care to even call up in my memory.

We pull bandanas over our noses and hustle away, the sounds of bones crunching under our boots.

We head to the northwest and scrounge at a home sitting alone in the flat desert. It's not much, a one-room building with an outhouse and a few junker cars in front.

We end up with a couple of cans of food and I get a jacket. I look as ridiculous as Dallas now in her pink down jacket. Mine is this puffy down thing that reaches past my butt and is a shocking yellow.

I don't plan to keep it any longer than I have to, but any jacket in an apocalypse.

Our slow walk over the desert towards Winslow is uneventful except for one thing. The pod.

About half an hour out, we spot it to the east of us a ways away as it meanders to the north. It's not close, there is no immediate danger, and without speaking we all stop and stare at it.

The land here has a bit more slope to it and the pod is higher than us, up on a low hill. The air is cool and fresh, my nose starting to wake up after being assaulted by the rotten moldy smell of Zs for so long.

I don't know why June and Dallas are staring, but I'm staring because I still can't believe it. Intelligent groups of zombies. I don't want to believe it. I want it to be different. So I stare.

"Shit," Dallas says, invoking the official word of the apocalypse. "I think they spotted us."

She's right. Their fresh-brains radar locks on and they change direction and start shambling towards us, the circle elongating and heading to the west like some ameba crawling around.

But we don't move. Not right away. We have time and I'm trying to think of strategies for dealing with them now that they seem to have a collective brain.

"We better go," June says, but her tone is tentative.

The pod slinks towards us for a minute and then it seems to hesitate. The pod looks to be experiencing some kind of internal chaos, some members moving towards us farther and some moving back the way they came, and some seemingly frozen.

"What the hell is it doing?" Dallas asks.

Zs don't act this way. They go for food with a single-minded brutality, and we are food.

The stretching out of the circle doesn't last long and soon they are all heading back the way they came, forming a tight circle again.

"What was that?" June asks.

"They just changed their mind," I say, the words slipping out before I thought them through, but that has to be it. Some individual Zs wanted to keep coming towards us and others didn't. It took a little bit for the group mind to come to a consensus.

"They're afraid of us," June says, and a chill runs down my spine despite my warm jacket.

For them to be afraid of us means that they had to have recognized us. Which means their zombie radar is more than just fresh-meat detection. It means they can differentiate individuals.

"Shit," I say, because there is nothing else to say.

"Can we get the hell out of here?" Dallas asks.

THE DESERT HERE IS BARREN. Bits of spring grass, short tufts of sage, and no trees, but visibility isn't bad, at least for the east side of town.

We're in what used to be Homolovi State Park perched up above the Little Colorado River, right outside of Winslow, just before dawn. We took our time because of Dallas's ankle and my energy and took the rest of yesterday and all night getting here. We are planning to stay in the Anasazi ruins today and observe Winslow. Find out if Talia is here. Try to get a sense of what she is up to.

We are more dedicated than ever to going back to the Grand Canyon. Not just to make a stand against Talia but to be in a place that is isolated and defensible. A place better suited to the new intelligent zombie group mind.

We are also here just trying to wrap our brains around what has happened in the last two weeks since we left the Grand Canyon, ran into Talia, and started playing her twisted game. The Apache Death Caves. The madness in Winslow with Dallas chained to the statue of Glenn Frey. My infection and recovery. The zombie siege in the cell tower treehouse. And now, the intelligent zombie pods.

"Contact in three... two... one..." Dallas says, the binoculars to her face, all three of us lying on the ground and peeking through some bushes at part of Winslow.

Dallas has our best binocs, some 10x50 Bushnell's we scrounged on the way here, the place she is looking at over a mile away and it's not easy to make out much, but it's as close as we dare get.

The zombie pod that headed west just hit town and a group of guards set up on Old Route 66 near the park where Talia blew up our truck.

Except the pod didn't just shamble in on the most direct route. It hesitated when it got close. When it's fresh-brains radar detected the living. It shambled off the road, over the train tracks, actually moving past the guards and then shambled back over the tracks, increased its speed, and descended on the small group of men from behind.

That is what Dallas is counting down. But the guards don't see the Zs right away. The three of them are sitting on the tailgate of their pickup truck playing cards, keeping an eye on the road, still convinced that all the Zs are gone, that the Zs are easy to spot, that the Zs are stupid.

The world has changed and they don't know it yet. Never a good formula for survival.

It doesn't last long. The guards see the Zs and start firing, one of them with something automatic, but it does no good. We don't see much, and we're too far away to hear the screams, but it doesn't take long.

The pod takes the guards out and finally get something to eat.

Dallas, who has been narrating all of this since June and I can't see shit, lowers the binoculars and is staring blankly and blinking too much. "I think we better go," she says. "I think we better find a roof or something to sleep on."

Her tone is flat, way too flat for Dallas, and even in the dim light I can tell that she's gone pale.

We've all seen people eaten by Zs, so I think it is the intelligence of the pod that has her freaked out this much.

"What about trying to find out if Talia is here?" I ask. That is the plan we agreed upon.

Dallas smiles vaguely. "Oh... I don't know. If she's here she has her hands full. Very full."

"Your ankle up for it?" June asks. We are about twenty miles out from the cell tower and I'm growing a whole new generation of blisters and don't want to walk anymore today.

"Sure," she says with another vague smile.

Gone is the flirty Dallas and gone are my own ruminations on relationships and what exactly to call what June and I have. I love her. I want to be with her. But this is a whole new thing we are dealing with now.

Survival comes first and we have determined that our best chance of survival is to return to the Grand Canyon. To see if we can make a stand there with the other survivors. Against Talia. Against the new intelligent zombie pods. A place where there is plenty of water and we can grow food. A place we ran away from just fourteen days ago.

June looks at me, her ocean-blue eyes questioning. She wants to know if I'm recovered enough from my illness, my infection. She, of course, is ready for more miles.

"Yeah," I say. "Let's keep going. Let's go where Talia least expects it."

We leave without another word, keeping low until we pass the bushes and out of sight of Winslow, and then we lengthen our strides and head out into the open desert.

June takes my hand and gives it a squeeze. I smile at her and enjoy the moment, and for once, don't overthink it.

"Knock, knock," Dallas says.

June catches my eye, her forehead wrinkling. "Who's there...?" she asks tentatively.

"Zombie," Dallas says.

"Zombie who?" I ask.

"Zombie pods suck," she says. "They really suck! Our gift to you Talia. I hope they eat your ugly face."

She raises her free middle finger back towards Winslow, and June and I laugh.

It wasn't a joke, not a real one, but it was our laughter for the day. And Dallas is back to being herself and we've got a plan and we've got each other.

We walk on, having no idea what will come next in Woody and June (and Dallas) versus the Apocalypse.

MORE ADVENTURE?

THERE IS SO MUCH MORE Woody and June (and Dallas too) coming. If you loved these stories (and if you got to the end here, I sure hope you did), please sign up for my newsletter at RobertJMcCarter.com/newsletter, and for bonus points, tell everyone you know! The more support these books get, the faster I'll get to writing the next volume.

When you subscribe to my newsletter you'll get a free 750+ page ebook, *Bits, Bites, and Rarities: The Worlds of Robert J. McCarter*, that introduces you to my many series, and has four stories you can't read anywhere else including "Park's Law of the Apocalypse," a novelette that takes place in the world of Woody and June.

Until then, remember that your life is an adventure and no matter what current "apocalypse" is befalling you, love hard, be kind, and take it all in stride.

While you wait, you might be interested in my superhero / love story series: *Neutrinoman & Lightningirl: A Love Story*. In this series I take a similar spin on the superhero genre as I did here with zombies. Real characters in extraordinary situations that are full of adventure, fun, and romance. Season 1 and 2 are out.. All the details are below

SUPERHEROES... FALLING IN LOVE... SAVING THE WORLD

Follow Nik Nichols (aka Neutrinoman) and Licia Lopez (aka Light-ningirl) on this wild adventure past "happily ever after" into the heart of love while they try to protect the Earth from aliens bent on our destruction.

Join my newsletter and get the first episode ebook, *Meteor Attack!*, for free!

Each episode is available separately, but buy a season at a time for the vest value.

Season 1: Episodes 1 - 3

- Meteor Attack!: Falling in love and saving the world...
- Toxic Asset: Friend or Enemy?
- Protocol X: An Alien Encounter

Season 2: Episodes 4 - 6

- Off Book: An impossible mission...
- Hard Times: Everything will change...
- Elemental Factors: A team arises

ABOUT THE AUTHOR

Robert J. McCarter is the author of more than ten novels and over a hundred short stories. He is a regular contributor to *Pulphouse Fiction Magazine* and his short fiction has also appeared in *The Saturday Evening Post, Andromeda Spaceways Inflight Magazine, Everyday Fiction,* and numerous anthologies.

Robert writes in a variety of genres from contemporary fantasy to science fiction and just about everything in between. His diverse background—including a career in software engineering, growing up on a ranch riding horses, and acting—colors the stories he tells.

He lives in the mountains of Arizona with his amazing wife and his ridiculously adorable dogs.

Find out more at:
RobertJMcCarter.com

BOOKS BY ROBERT J. MCCARTER

WOODY AND JUNE VERSUS THE APOCALYPSE

For a great deal, pick up *Woody and June Versus the Apocalypse* a volume at at time!

Woody and June Versus the Apocalypse: Volume 1 (Episodes 1 - 7)

- Woody and June versus the Wannabe Warlord
- Woody and June versus the Fungus-Head Zombies
- Woody and June versus the Grand Canyon
- Woody and June versus the Ex
- Woody and June versus the Third Wheel
- Woody and June versus Phantom Company
- Woody and June versus the Daring Rescue

Woody and June Versus the Apocalypse: Volume 2 (Episodes 8 - 12) *Coming 2/2023*

- Woody and June versus the Chase (coming 9/2022)
- Woody and June versus Two Guns (coming 10/2022)
- Woody and June versus Winslow (coming 11/2022)
- Woody and June versus the Infection (coming 12/2022)
- Woody and June versus the Siege (coming 1/2023)

Find out more at WoodyAndJune.com

For a great deal, pick up *Neutrinoman & Lightningirl: A Love Story* a season at at time!

Season 1 (Omnibus edition of Episodes 1 - 3)

- Meteor Attack!
- Toxic Asset
- Protocol X

Season 2 (Omnibus edition of Episodes 4-6)

- Off Book
- Hard Times
- Elemental Factors

Find out the latest at Neutrinoman.com

For a complete list of books, go to RobertJMcCarter.com/books